Charlotte Helms had stormed into his life like some badass angel of justice, shaking up his quiet, orderly world.

"Do you have a girlfriend or—" her face tightened "—a wife?"

"Nope." He'd had a fiancée this time last year, but Ashley had brushed him off with a Dear John letter while he was in Afghanistan. Not that he could blame her frustration with his absence, but it rankled. Last he'd heard, she was already engaged to another man.

"What about you?" He'd assumed she wasn't married, but what did he really know about her?

She snorted. "Hell, no."

Irrational relief flowed over him.

"My profession doesn't exactly lend itself to maintaining close, personal relationships," she continued. "Haven't even seen my own parents in months."

"That must be hard."

"Yeah, it's tough." Charlotte sighed and ran a hand through her long hair. "It never used to bother me, but lately..."

APPALACHIAN ABDUCTION

—

DEBBIE HERBERT

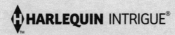

This book is dedicated to all my author friends who help me,
especially: Gwen Knight, Lexi George, Ash Fitzsimmons,
Michelle Edwards, Tammy Lynn, Fran Holland and Audrey Jordan!

And, as always, to my husband, Tim, my dad, J.W. Gainey,
and my sons, Byron and Jacob.

ISBN-13: 978-1-335-63906-6

Appalachian Abduction

Copyright © 2018 by Debbie Herbert

Recycling programs
for this product may
not exist in your area.

Printed in U.S.A.

www.Harlequin.com

Debbie Herbert writes paranormal and romantic suspense novels reflecting her belief that love, like magic, casts its own spell of enchantment. A 2017 Rita finalist, she's always been fascinated by magic, romance and gothic stories. Married and living in Alabama, she roots for the Crimson Tide football team. Her eldest son, like many of her characters, has autism. Her youngest son is in the US Army. A past Maggie Award finalist in both young adult and paranormal romance, she loves to hear from readers!

Books by Debbie Herbert

Harlequin Intrigue

Appalachian Prey
Appalachian Abduction

Harlequin Nocturne

Bayou Magic

Bayou Shadow Hunter
Bayou Shadow Protector
Bayou Wolf

Dark Seas

Siren's Secret
Siren's Treasure
Siren's Call

Visit the Author Profile page at Harlequin.com.

CAST OF CHARACTERS

Charlotte Helms—A dedicated undercover cop who's traveled to the north Georgia mountains to help a young girl escape from a human-trafficking ring. She trusts no one, not even the small-town deputy whose help she needs to find the victim.

James Tedder—After returning from his last military deployment, he wants nothing more than to settle down to small-town life as a deputy sheriff. He suffers from PTSD and has withdrawn from close relationships—until the fiery redhead arrives in town. She's an enticing mystery, one he would love to solve.

Maddie and Richard Stowers—A rich couple from Atlanta who own a luxurious cabin in the exclusive Falling Rock community on Blood Mountain. They're respected members of the community, so no one believes that behind their closed doors at the luxury mountain retreat there might be young girls imprisoned for the human-trafficking trade.

Chapter One

Only one road climbed Blood Mountain to the exclusive Falling Rock community and its luxury mansions. But Charlotte had no interest in accessing the gated community through the pretty lane lined with oaks and vistas of manicured lawns and gardens.

No, the backside view of the swanky neighborhood was where she'd find clues to the ugly mystery of Jenny's whereabouts. And to get to this precious vantage point in the hollow, she'd hiked a good two miles down from neighboring Lavender Mountain. She raised her binoculars and focused on the nearest cabin's massive wooden deck.

Nobody milling about there.

She slanted them to the cabin's impressive wall of windows, hoping to catch a glimpse of Jenny—or any other young teenage girl, for that matter. The bastards.

Still nothing.

But she wasn't discouraged. If nothing else, her career as an undercover cop had taught her patience. She waited and, after a few minutes, scanned the row of houses yet again before dropping the binoculars and taking a swig from her water bottle.

Faint voices rumbled through the air, low, deep and indecipherable. Quickly she raised the binoculars to search for the source. But the field glasses weren't necessary. Near the base of the cabin, only one hundred yards away, stood two men armed with shotguns and wearing walkie-talkies belted at their waists. Where had they come from?

Suddenly the muscular guy on the left raised an arm and pointed a pair of binoculars at *her*.

Oh, no.

She'd been spotted, despite the fact that she was dressed in camouflage and had tucked her red hair into an olive ski cap. The man on the right raised a shotgun to his shoulder and scanned the area. Charlotte dropped to the ground on her stomach, praying she was out of sight. Three deep breaths, and she raised her binoculars again. The men had disappeared.

Strangely, she wasn't comforted by that realization. They could be creeping their way downhill to find her. Time to get the heck out of Dodge. Charlotte tucked the binoculars and water bottle into her backpack and withdrew her pistol. Not the standard-issue one provided by the Atlanta Police Department—they'd forced her to turn that in—but the personal one she always kept stashed in her nightstand. If they found her, she'd be ready for them. The cool, hard wood snuggled in her right hand provided a surge of comfort, just as it always had on those nights when she'd been home alone and whispers of danger made her imagine some ex-con had discovered where she lived.

Charlotte eased the backpack onto her shoulders. Cocking her head to the side, she paused, listening for anything out of the ordinary.

Wind moaned through the trees, and dead leaves gusted in noisy spirals. Then she heard it: a methodical crunching of the forest underbrush that thickly carpeted the ground. At least one of the men was headed her way.

Damn it.

She jumped to her feet and ran, heart savagely skittering. Its pounding beat pulsed in her ears, loud as the echo of dynamite. A slug whistled high above her, and bark exploded from near the top of a pine sapling eight feet ahead.

Did they mean to kill her or merely frighten her off? Because if their aim was the latter, it was working. Charlotte kept running, this time darting behind trees every ten yards or so. No sense providing them with an easy target. The path seemed to stretch on forever, though, and a stitch in her side finally screamed in protest at the brisk pace. Charlotte stumbled behind a wide oak and sucked oxygen into her burning lungs.

Another shot rent the air, but she couldn't tell where the bullet landed. Hopefully not anywhere nearby. She pushed off and ran once more. Wind blasted her ears and cheeks, stinging her eyes as she sped down the trail, mentally calculating her best escape. If only she knew how close they were.

There were three options. One, return to the nearby abandoned cabin and hope they didn't see her sneak inside. Two, if there was enough time, hightail it to her truck hidden in a copse of trees and take off. The problem with the first two was that her cover might be compromised if she were spotted. The third option was riskier, but it would leave her free to continue her planned surveillance.

Another shot torpedoed by like an angry hornet, grazing the side of a nearby oak. This shot was much closer. Again, she ran. Gnarled roots gripped her right foot and she fell flat. A pained cry slipped past her lips. She stared down at her twisted knee and the ripped denim on the outside of her right thigh where brambles and rocks had cut deep. Blood oozed and created a widening stain on her pants. Her right temple throbbed and she knew a knot would form on her scalp. Charlotte swallowed hard, pushing back the sudden stab of dizziness that narrowed her vision. No allowing the blessed relief of unconsciousness to take hold. The things men like them could do…she'd seen way too many victims and knew a thousand ways evil people could inflict pain upon another.

Focus. You can't let them catch you.

Option three it was, then. Quickly she ripped off her jacket and pressed it against her wound. Couldn't let blood drip to the ground and become a trail that would lead the men to her. Not to mention the danger of passing out from blood loss.

She hissed at the wave of pain that slammed into her knee. It was as if someone had tripped a live wire inside her that burned through her veins and traveled up and down her body. Even her mouth had a metallic, coppery taste. Charlotte spit a mouthful of blood, clamped her teeth shut and crouched low. Plenty of time later to moan and groan. Right now she had to find cover.

It hurt like hell, but she managed a stumbling trot, forsaking the main path and stumbling through shrubs and bands of trees. Winter was a hell of a time to seek shelter in the Appalachian forest. The plants were practically stripped bare, their only foliage a few withered, stubborn leaves that had not yet broken loose. But there were patches of evergreen shrubs and small pine trees still to be found. She'd checked on that in her earlier recon of the area.

"Where'd he go?" one of the men shouted from afar.

The answering voice was much closer. "Lost sight of him."

She dove behind a clump of rhododendrons and curled into a tight ball. If they hadn't seen her, she had a chance. Her breath sawed in and out—to her ears, loud enough to doom any hope of going unnoticed. She crossed her left hand over her thigh and pressed down on the wound to staunch the bleeding. Those damn briars ripped flesh like tiny surgical knives. The pistol was in her right hand, loaded, with the safety off. If they came too close and found her hidey-hole, she might be able to fire at them first.

They tromped through the area and continued the search. Subtlety wasn't their strength.

"You go that way," one of them shouted, pointing in the opposite direction, "and I'll head this way."

A tide of relief whooshed through her body. One would be easier than two if it came to a showdown.

Footsteps approached, and she rounded into herself even tighter, not daring to breathe.

Please don't stop. Keep walking, she prayed as the nearest man stomped not twenty yards away. He wore black leather boots and dark denims—that much she could see—but she didn't dare lift her face and examine him further.

He stumbled on a rock and tumbled forward several steps, managing to catch his balance at the last minute. "Damn it," he snarled, then yelled, "Anyone out there?"

Right. Like she was going to raise her hand and pop up like a jack-in-the-box to answer him.

"If you can hear me, you were trespassing. Stay away from Falling Rock, got it? Hey, Ricky, let's get back to the house," he called to his fellow tracker, then walked back toward the main trail.

Another voice, deeper and more gravelly, spoke. "Probably just a hunter, anyway."

"I didn't see no shotgun on him, but he was wearing camouflage. Scrawny little fella."

"Might not have been hunting animals. Could be one of them 'sengers."

What the heck was a 'senger? Whatever they were, she was grateful they provided another plausible explanation for a person roaming the woods in camouflage attire.

Her breathing slowed at the sound of receding

footsteps. Today had almost been disastrous, and she wasn't in the clear yet.

If those men were smart, they'd linger a bit, hoping that their prey would be cocky enough, or stupid enough, to reemerge on the trail, mistakenly believing the danger had passed. But six years on the force had honed her methods and instincts. *Never believe your opponent isn't as smart, or smarter, than yourself*, she'd been warned.

And so she waited. As shock and adrenaline faded, the pain in her knee and temple increased. As soon as she got to the cabin, she'd clean the wound and patch it up with the first aid kit she'd brought along. She also had Ace bandages to wrap her knee. It had to be a superficial injury, since she'd been able to put weight on her leg and run. The air chilled her skin, although not enough to counteract the burn of ripped flesh. Were the men still lying in wait? She wasn't sure how much longer she could stay. Every moment the wound went unattended increased the likelihood of infection, and she desperately wanted to take something for the building headache.

Gingerly Charlotte rose and tested putting weight on her right leg. A bolt of pain traveled up from her knee, and she bit her lip to keep from crying out. Hurt or not, she had to leave. Those men might return with a larger force. And even if her damn cell phone worked out here in the boonies, who could she call? Right now, she was a pariah to her coworkers, and if she called the local authorities, they'd pepper her with questions.

She gripped her pistol more tightly and set off toward the main trail. Once she got there, she'd walk along the outskirts until she was sure the men were truly gone.

The trail looked as forlorn and barren as when she'd first hiked it that morning. Charlotte ran a hand through her hair and then stopped cold. At some point, her hat had been blown away by the wind. Good thing the men were gone. Now she needed to push through the pain and walk. She could do that. There was no choice.

It appeared she'd survived this encounter. Sometimes the best option was to hide and live to fight another day. Justice delayed beat justice denied. Besides, it wasn't as if she harbored a death wish, though death would be preferable to what these men were capable of doing.

They might have succeeded in running her off for the day, but she wasn't giving up. She couldn't give up. Not today, not ever. She was the last, best hope for Jenny and the other lost girls.

THE NEAR-DESERTED roads suited James just fine. October, while beautiful in the Appalachians, had drawn crowds of tourists flocking to view the scenic foliage. But November's gray skies and biting wind meant that Lavender Mountain was back to its usual calmness—and he could sure use some peace and quiet. Returning from Afghanistan hadn't exactly led to the grand family homecoming he'd once envisioned. Instead, murder had wiped out half his family before he'd even set foot in Elmore County. That tragedy, combined with what the doctors deemed a mild case of PTSD, had left him edgy and filled with uncertainty about the future.

With no conscious plan, James meandered the deputy sheriff's cruiser up the mountain road, and he startled at the sudden sight of his father's old cabin. How often had he done this very thing on routine patrols? Ended up driving right here, precisely at the place he'd rather *not* be?

He shook his head in disgust and hit the accelerator. Memory Lane had zip appeal.

Twenty yards down the road, a flash of beige slashed through his peripheral vision. What was that? He did a U-turn and craned his neck, searching the brown-and-gray woods. *There*, he spotted it again. Curious, he pulled onto his father's old property and exited the cruiser, shrugging into his jacket. He strode along the tree line until he solved the riddle: someone had parked their truck toward the back of the property behind a couple of large trees. He retrieved his cell phone and hurried over on the off chance that someone might be injured or stranded.

It was locked, but he peered in the tinted windows. No clues there. The interior was practically empty and spotlessly clean. He headed to the back of the truck and took a photo of the license plate. He'd call in the numbers shortly.

No damn reason it should be here. No *good* reason, anyway. Frowning, he went to the cabin and pulled out his keys. Better make sure some squatter hadn't decided to take up free residence.

He inserted the key in the lock, but it wouldn't turn. James withdrew it and checked—yes, this was the correct key. Someone had changed the locks. He felt a prickle of unease mixed with anger, and the twin emotions churned in his gut. Anger won.

"Open up," he bellowed, rapping his knuckles on the old wooden door. "Sheriff's department."

Silence.

He stepped back on the porch and noticed for the first time that every window was taped up with plain brown wrapping paper. This was *his* place, damn it. He'd chosen not to live in the cabin he'd inherited, but that didn't mean just anyone could help themselves to it and move in. James rapped on the door again, louder. "Open up now, or I'll break down the door."

Still no answer.

With a quick burst of energy, he kicked the door. Splinters flew, and the frame rattled. He kicked again, and it burst open. James shuffled to the side and removed his sidearm, then proceeded cautiously inside with his gun raised. The room was abnormally dark from the taped windows, and only the light from the open doorway illuminated the den. At least his sister had gotten rid of most of the furniture. In this room, only an old couch remained. No place to hide.

James flicked the light switch, grateful he'd kept the power on. The Realtor had insisted on it so she could show the place to potential buyers. *That* was a laugh—the place had sat empty for months. Seemed fixer-upper cabins in remote Appalachia weren't a hot commodity. Hardly a shocker.

He made his way to the kitchen, gun still drawn. Like the truck and the den, it was pristine, and mostly empty. No signs of forced entry or habitation. Three more rooms to check. He padded down the short hallway, gun at the ready. The guest bedroom and bathroom doors stood open, but the main bedroom door was shut.

Gotcha, he almost whispered aloud. He spared a cursory glance in the guest room that housed only a bed. Nothing was underneath the tucked comforter, so he eased toward the closed door.

Spots of spilled liquid, still wet, stained the pine flooring leading from the bedroom into the bathroom. He flipped on the bathroom switch, careful to keep his gun aimed at the closed bedroom door.

Smeared blood and dirt formed a drag pattern on the floor and basin and continued their path to the side of the tub. A wet towel lay beside the tub, as well as strips of gauze and a bottle of rubbing alcohol. Someone had been hurt—and recently.

A grating metal sound came from behind the closed bedroom door, and James barreled into the room. A mattress lay on the floor, and food provisions and clothes were neatly stacked in plastic containers along the side wall. But it was the open window that drew his immediate focus. Oh, *hell* no, they weren't slipping away. He was going to get answers. James rushed to the window and stuck his head out.

Red hair whipped in the breeze. A petite woman wearing a camouflage shirt and black panties—no pants, no shoes—ran through the yard. Blood oozed from ripped flesh on her right leg, and she limped as she headed toward the truck.

Okay, that was far from the thug or drugged-out squatter he'd expected. "Halt," he ordered.

She didn't even bother looking back at him as she continued a gimpy run to the tree line.

"For Christ's sake," he muttered, tucking his sidearm back into its holster and rushing through the cabin. He exited the busted front door and stormed down the porch steps to the side yard. "Stop right now," he called out.

Again she ignored his command. Stubborn, foolish woman. He couldn't let her get in that truck. But as he ran toward her, she spun around, raising a pistol in both hands and aiming it straight at his heart.

James threw up his hands and cautiously walked forward before pointing at his badge. "Lady, you don't want to shoot an officer of the law." He nodded at her leg. "Looks like you need medical attention."

"You're a cop? Let me take a look at that badge." She approached and examined the badge on his uniform. The harsh glint in her eyes softened, and she lowered the gun. "Sorry. I didn't stop to see who broke in when I ran."

"I identified myself as from the *Sheriff's department*," he said grimly. She might be pretty as all get-out and pretend compliance, but people weren't always what they seemed. This job and his tour of duty had taught him those lessons well. "Now gently lay down the gun and step away from it," he ordered.

She kept her eyes on him as she bent her knees

and placed her weapon on the ground. "No problem, Officer. I always—"

Her right leg gave out from underneath, and she swooned forward—which put her hands right by her gun, he couldn't help noticing. Quickly he crossed the distance between them and kicked it several yards away.

"Suspicious much?" she drawled.

"I'll call for an ambulance or drive you to the hospital in my vehicle. Do you have a preference?"

"Neither. I'm fine. It's not as bad as it looks."

"There's blood on the right side of your scalp. Not to mention your mangled leg. Might need stitches, at the very least. Antibiotics, too."

"I said no." She struggled to stand and then limped past him. "Just let me get dressed."

"Not until you explain how you got hurt and what you were doing in my cabin."

That got through to the woman, and she whirled around. "*Your* cabin?" She bit her lip and mumbled, "Of all the damn luck."

"You can explain on the way to the hospital."

"I don't need a doctor."

She hobbled to the door, and he scrambled to retrieve the fallen weapon before following her, trying to deduce this stranger's game. "You hiding from an abusive husband?" he guessed.

"No," she said flatly, grabbing onto the porch rail and wincing as she climbed the steps.

"There are shelters that can help, you know. In fact, there's one less than thirty miles—"

"I don't need a shelter. I can protect myself."

Like hell she could. "Fine. You want to clam up? Let's go down to the station. I'll run your license plate and clear up this mystery."

She sighed, resignation rounding her shoulders. "If you don't mind, I'd like to get my clothes on."

Woman was probably freezing her butt off. "Of course. Look, whatever kind of trouble you're in, we can help."

She blinked and nodded her head. "Thank you, Officer. I'm sorry about intruding and… and pulling that gun on you."

About time she saw sense. "Fine. I'll wait here." He took in her pale face, and his eyes traveled down to her right leg. "Can you manage by yourself?" he asked gruffly.

"Of course. Any chance I can have my gun back now? After you unload it, of course."

What kind of fool did she think he was? "No, you may not."

She cast her eyes down in a demure manner. "Be back in a minute."

He watched as she made her faltering way down the hall, her back ramrod straight. What kind of man could hurt a woman that way? It looked as though she'd taken a hard tumble. Her ex was obviously dangerous. He'd see that whoever the man was, he'd get his due punishment.

James paced the empty den, thinking of his dad and sister Darla, both murdered at the hands of another family member. How sad that the ones we most loved were often our worst enemies and betrayers of our trust.

He shook his head and strode to the windows, stripping off the papers the woman had taped up to avoid detection. It shouldn't matter, but he hated the thought of the cabin being shrouded in darkness night and day. Bad enough he'd abandoned it to die a slow death from neglect.

What was taking her so long? Had she passed out from loss of blood?

A flash of red in the barren landscape caught his eye.

Damn it to hell. She was running away again, this time fully clothed and with a backpack strapped to her shoulders.

Should have known the minute he'd seen those teal eyes and titian-colored hair that this woman spelled trouble.

Chapter Two

Charlotte suppressed a wince as she collapsed into the seat across from his desk at the Lavender Mountain Sheriff's Office. She glanced at his nameplate. Officer James Tedder. The name had a familiar ring.

"Driver's license, please," he said matter-of-factly, firing up the computer on his battered wooden desk. He examined her gun and wrote down the serial number before opening his desk drawer and locking it away.

"License. Right." She made a show of rummaging through her backpack. "Shoot," she mumbled. "It's not here. Must have left it at the cabin. Sorry."

He quirked a brow. "How convenient. Tell me your name."

The officer was bound to get her real name from the truck's license plate numbers. No use lying. "Charlotte Helms."

He picked up his cell phone, and she saw a

photo of the rental tag as he typed. But there was no need to panic just because he had her name. He'd run a standard background check and see she had no priors. No reason for him to look further and check out her employment record. A little fast talking on her part to avoid trespassing charges, and her cover would remain uncompromised.

"The truck's a rental," she volunteered. "Thought it would be easier to keep my ex-boy-friend off the trail that way." She trembled her lips and let her eyes fill with tears. This wouldn't be her first performance for getting out of a jam. And acting was so much easier when she actually felt like crying from pain. "You were right. I'm running from someone."

"How did you wind up in my cabin?"

Bad spot of luck there. It'd looked perfect when she'd scouted the area earlier—practically deserted but sturdy, and the location so close to Falling Rock. She'd figured it would be less conspicuous to camp there than to rent a room at a local motel. The tourist season was long over and she didn't want to attract attention.

"It…seemed safe," she hedged. "I was afraid if I stayed at a motel he'd track me down. I don't have much cash on me, only credit cards." She added a hitch to her voice. "I left in a bit of a hurry."

He paused a heartbeat, drumming his fingers on the desk. "How did he hurt you?"

His face and voice were neutral and she couldn't tell if he was buying her story or not. Charlotte thought fast.

"It wasn't my ex-boyfriend. I'd gone for a walk," she lied. "Got a little stir crazy holed up in the cabin. I must have ended up on someone's property because a shot came out of nowhere. Might have been an irate land owner. Or…maybe it was a hunter mistaking me for a deer? I didn't stick around to find out. In my hurry, I stumbled and took a hard fall."

"Exactly where were you when this incident occurred?"

"About a mile or two south of the cabin? I can't say. I was focused on getting the hell out of there."

A *ding* sounded on the computer and he turned to the screen. "Truck was rented from Atlanta," he read. "Two days ago. The contract states you've rented it for two weeks."

"That's right." Charlotte swiped at her eyes and sniffed. "I apologize for staying at your cabin. I'll be glad to pay for a new door and any other damages incurred."

He leaned back in his chair and steepled his fingers. "A crime's been committed here."

"Please don't arrest me for trespassing. I've

never been in trouble with the law." Then she remembered. "And, um, sorry for that other incident, too."

"You drew a gun on me," he stated flatly, a muscle flexing in his jaw.

"I thought you were my ex."

"Again, I identified myself before entering the cabin. Fleeing an officer is a crime."

"But I didn't *see* you," she argued. "I couldn't be sure who you really were."

"And then there's the matter of someone taking potshots at you. I'm going to need more details on that."

She waved a hand in the air dismissively. "Why? I'm fine. I won't be pressing charges even if you find the one who fired. I just want to move on. I decided during that long walk today that I want to stay with my parents in South Carolina for a bit. Get my life together and put distance between me and my ex."

"Move on all you like, but I still have the problem of a rogue shooter in the woods. We're going back there and you're going to show me where you were when this happened."

"But…my leg."

"You claim the injury's not serious enough for medical attention."

Her temper rose. "But I can't walk a mile and go scouting around the wilderness."

"I have a four-wheeler. You won't have to walk."

"I see." She cleared her throat and pressed a hand to her head injury. "Could we do this tomorrow?"

His blank expression never wavered. "You have a permit to carry a weapon?"

Charlotte blinked at the sudden change of topic. The damn gun. Once he ran the serial numbers he'd have her employment history. And then her cover was blown.

"Of course I have a permit."

If only she could be sure he was a clean cop. It would be amazing to have assistance in saving Jenny. And he acted sincere with his direct manner. His face was rugged while at the same time maintaining a certain boyish charm. She couldn't deny that she found him appealing and his forthright air inexplicably tugged at her to confide everything. But this was a small town, one that Jenny Ashbury's kidnappers had chosen for a reason. And that reason might very well be that local law enforcement had been paid to turn a blind eye on the abductor's comings and goings.

She couldn't take that chance with Jenny's life.

A middle-aged lady with dark hair and bifocals stuck her head in the door. "Harlan needs to speak with you ASAP."

Officer Tedder frowned. "Can't it wait?"

"Nope."

Charlotte's paranoia radar activated. Harlan Sampson was the county sheriff. Was there any way he knew who she was and why she was here? Was that why he wanted to speak with Officer Tedder?

"Be right back," he said.

Alone, Charlotte leaned over the desk and peeked at the computer screen. Her not-so-flattering driver's license photo was on display. Feeling restless, she stood and strolled to the open window, wincing at the burst of pain.

Downtown Lavender Mountain was picturesque with its gift shops and cafés. From here she could see the local coffee shop and a gourmet cheese store. Despite the off season, a few people were out and about.

Leave. Just leave. Now.

Charlotte bit her lip, debating the wisdom of her inner voice. It's not like Officer Tedder had arrested her, right? And he didn't issue an order to stay when he left. If she could keep out of sight for a couple of hours and then hitch a ride back to her truck, maybe he'd give up on questioning her.

Yeah…but then what? Stay the next town over? It wouldn't be as convenient, but she could rent a different vehicle, find an inconspicuous place to park it near Falling Rock, and then continue on as before. All it took was one photograph of any of the lost girls by a window, one slip-up by the kidnappers transporting their captives, or one girl to escape their cabin and make a run for it. Then she'd have the needed proof to obtain a search warrant and rescue Jenny.

It was worth the risk. Hell, she'd already damaged her career by coming to Lavender Mountain anyway. So what if a local cop got angry with her and eventually charged her with trespassing? That was the least of her worries.

With a longing glance at the locked drawer housing her gun, Charlotte scooped up her backpack. She'd get another weapon. If nothing else, she was resourceful and a risk-taker. With that, and a whole lot of luck, she'd bring down that human trafficking ring.

SOMETHING ABOUT HER story didn't jibe. James hurried back to his office. More than anyone, he realized these mountains were as dangerous a place as any city. He need look no further than his own family for confirmation of that sad fact. But hunters shooting at a woman didn't sound right. Hunters around these parts knew you shot by sight, not sound. Was it an irate property owner? It was possible they'd fired a warning shot or two in the air. People 'round these parts didn't take kindly to trespassers on their land.

And what was she so afraid of? If Charlotte Helms could afford to rent a truck, she could afford a motel. No reason an ex from Atlanta would ever think to look in this area.

Time for answers.

Squaring his shoulders, he stepped back into his office. His empty office. No, surely she didn't run again. She wouldn't, would she?

"Sammy," he bellowed, scurrying down the hall.

"What's up?" Samuel Armstrong asked, not looking up from his computer.

"Did you see a woman leave the building a minute ago? A redhead limping on her right leg?"

"Nah," he drawled with a wry grin. "Saw y'all come in, though. You manage to lose her?"

"Maybe." James hurried over to Zelda's cubicle. "Did you see that woman in my office leave?"

Zelda laid down her pencil and crossword puzzle book. "No, my back's been to the door. Want me to check the ladies' room?"

"Please."

She rose from her chair with a sigh. He followed Harlan's secretary to the lobby restroom. But he guessed Zelda's answer before she emerged half a minute later.

"She's gone."

Aggravating woman. "Thanks," he mumbled,

hurrying back to his office for his jacket. He pulled it on as he rushed out of the lobby. He'd spoken with Harlan about five minutes, tops. Charlotte couldn't have gone far with an injured leg and no vehicle. He glanced up and down the road, but no flash of red was in sight. James crossed the street and entered the coffee shop. This was as good a place to start as any.

Myrtle waved as he entered. "What'll it be, Jim Bob? Your regular with two sugars and one cream?"

His campaign to have people address him as James instead of his boyhood nickname was not a success. "No, I'm looking for a woman. A petite redhead. Seen her?"

"You have very particular tastes," Myrtle said with a wink. "Didn't know you were partial to redheads and leather."

He was *so* not in the mood for jokes. "Sheriff's business. Has she been here or not?"

"Touchy today, huh? Nope, haven't seen your mysterious lady."

"Call me if you do."

He exited the shop and tried half a dozen others. No one had seen Charlotte. He stood in the middle of town square, hands on hips. Every minute that went by increased the likelihood that she'd succeeded in giving him the slip. *Think.* Where would he go if he were in her shoes?

Probably slink around the alleys and slip into a shop's back door if someone approached. He hustled behind the coffee shop and scanned the alley lined with garbage bins. Down at the far end, he spotted Charlotte rounding a corner, red hair flaming like a beacon.

I've got you now, he thought with grim satisfaction. He hurried to the end of the backstreet in time to see her slip into the Dixie Diner.

Now he'd get answers.

Inside the diner, the aroma of fried chicken, biscuits and gravy made his mouth water. Chasing Charlotte was hard work and it was past lunchtime. He scanned the tables filled with families.

No Charlotte.

He proceeded to the back exit and stuck his head out to check the alleyway.

Still no Charlotte.

Only one place left unchecked. He rapped on the ladies' room door once and then entered.

Lucille Bozeman, an elderly member of the local Red Hat Society, shrieked and clutched her pearls. "James Robert Tedder," she said breathlessly, "what on earth do you think you are doing?"

At least she'd used his full name instead of Jim Bob. Normally, he found her and the other members of the Red Hats a hoot—amusing older ladies with their red hats, purple attire and care-free spirit. But not today. Heat traveled up the nape of his neck. "Sorry, Mrs. Bozeman. I'm looking for a woman."

"You've come to the right place, but this is hardly appropriate behavior. I'll speak to Harlan Sampson about this. How dare you…"

But he tuned her out and bent over. No feet were visible under the stalls, but one door was closed. He knocked on it.

"Come on out, ma'am."

A long sigh, and then a dry voice answered. "You going to order me to put my hands up or you'll shoot?"

"I don't think that'll be necessary," he answered in kind. "Unless you try to flee from an officer of the law again."

Charlotte emerged with a wry smile and leaned against the wall, arms folded. "Sorry. You never arrested me so I'd assumed I was free to leave earlier."

Despite her flippant attitude, James noted that her face had paled and her eyes were slightly glazed. "Right. So that's why you ran and tried to give me the slip." He nodded at the bump on her head. "You might be concussed. Change your mind about going to the hospital to have that looked at?"

"Not at all. I'm fine."

"Are you in some kind of trouble, young lady?" Lucille walked over, the brim of her outlandish purple hat brushing against his shoulders. Her gaze swept Charlotte from head to toe. "You appear a mite peaked."

Charlotte's smile was tight. "Just a few superficial wounds."

"Jim Bob, you should take her to see Miss Glory. She's a sight better helping folks than any doctor."

Actually, that wasn't a bad idea—and the healer's shop was only two doors down.

He addressed Charlotte. "What do you say? No forms to fill out or insurance cards to process."

"All I need is over-the-counter pain medication. If you could point me in the direction of the local pharmacy?" She pushed past them both and made for the bathroom door.

James took her arm. "You're coming with me. Stop being so stubborn. It's obvious you're hurt. Miss Glory can fix you right up."

He caught a glimpse of Lucille gaping at them in the bathroom mirror. News of this bathroom encounter would be all over town in an hour.

"Thanks for the suggestion, Mrs. Bozeman." He leaned into Charlotte, whispering in her ear, "If you don't want your business common knowledge, let's continue this outside."

He stayed near her as they walked through the diner. Charlotte briefly glanced at every face in the crowd, as if taking their measure. She opened the door and stumbled, pitching forward a half step. The full weight of her body leaned against him. She smelled like some kind of flower—a rose, perhaps. It was as though a touch of spring had breathed life into a dreary November day.

Charlotte stiffened and drew back. A prickly rose, this one—beautiful but full of thorns. James clenched his jaw. Didn't matter how she looked or smelled or felt. This woman was a whole host of complications he didn't need or want. He'd get her medical attention, find out why she came to Lavender Mountain and then escort her to her truck and wish her well.

"If you're on the run as you claim, the last thing you want is an infection to set in that injury. Miss Glory really can help you."

"If I agree, will you give me a ride to my truck afterward and let me go?"

"You're in no position to negotiate. You trespassed on my property and pointed a gun at me, as well. I believe I'm holding the trump card."

"Okay, okay," she muttered.

She hobbled beside him until they reached the store.

Miss Glory's shop, The Root Worker, was dark. Glory claimed the light deteriorated the herbs strung along the rafters. The placed smelled like chamomile and always reminded him of the time he and his sisters, Darla and Lilah, had all come down with the flu at the same time. Their mother had infused the small cabin with a medicinal tonic provided by Miss Glory.

"What brings you here today, Jim Bob?" Glory asked, grinding herbs with a mortar and pestle. She swiped at the gray fringe of hair on her forehead. Her deeply lined face focused on Charlotte. "And who's your friend?"

James quickly made introductions. "She's here because of a lump on her head, a twisted knee and cut skin on her right thigh. She refuses to see a doctor, so I thought I'd bring her to you."

Glory didn't even blink an eye. No telling how many strange stories she'd heard over the years.

"I've already cleaned it out and bandaged it," Charlotte said. "Don't see the need for anything else."

"How bad do your injuries hurt?" Glory asked gently.

"I wouldn't turn down some aspirin."

"Hope you're not so stubborn that you ignore any signs of a concussion or infection. You start runnin' a fever or see red streaks flame out from the flesh, you get to a doctor quick, ya hear?"

Surprisingly, Charlotte nodded her head slightly. "I will."

"You seein' double or got the collywobbles in yer tummy?"

"None of that."

Every moment he spent in her company, his doubts about her story grew. He remembered her steady aim and fierce eyes as she aimed a gun dead center on his chest. This wasn't a woman who ran away from danger. She'd confront it head-on.

"Tell you what I'm gonna do, darlin'. I'm sending you home with a gallon of my sassafras tea. You drink a big ole glass of it at least three times a day. That sassafras is my special tonic that'll clear up any nasty germs brewing in yer body."

Miss Glory went behind the counter and rummaged a few moments, returning with a couple of items.

"A little poultice to draw out infection," she said, pressing it into Charlotte's palm. "And a few capsules filled with feverfew, devil's claw and a couple other goodies. Much better than an ole aspirin."

Charlotte shook her head. "I don't—"

"Now don't you fight me on this, child. I see the pain in them eyes of yers. You'll need a sharp mind to be of any use to anyone and you can't have that without rest. Take it before you go to bed at night."

"Thank you," Charlotte murmured, stuffing the poultice and pain packet in her backpack.

"Jim Bob, grab a gallon jug of sassafras tea on yer way out. It's in the cooler by the door." Glory rested an arthritic-weathered hand on Charlotte's shoulder. "I see danger surrounding you, child. They's people wish you would go away from here and never come back."

James was used to Miss Glory's eerie predictions. He wasn't sure he believed in all that hocus-pocus, but people around here claimed she had the sight. Couldn't hurt to pick her brain. "What do you know?" he asked sharply.

"Me?" She threw up her hands and cackled. "I'm just an old woman who's been around too many years to remember, and can sense people's energy."

He was reading too much into the old lady's ramblings. Wouldn't have even bothered coming to her shop, but Lilah swore that Miss Glory was the only one who helped her get through a difficult pregnancy and then again helped with her colicky baby.

Charlotte backed away to the door, suspicion hardening her classical features. "Who am I in danger from?" she asked sharply.

"That's not for me to say. But I suspect you know the answer to your own question."

Charlotte nodded and continued edging to the door.

He wasn't going to let her run again. James plopped down a couple twenties on the counter. "Will that cover everything?"

Miss Glory nodded and leaned in, her breath a whisper against his ear. "Watch after her. She needs help whether she likes it or not."

James shook his head. "I'm no one's protector," he grumbled. He had his own demons to fight. His tour of duty overseas had left him unwilling to get involved in others' problems, beyond what was required as an officer. Lilah often fussed that he'd become too withdrawn. But whatever—all he wanted was to perform his duties and be left alone.

Charlotte gasped suddenly and flung herself against the side wall, away from the shop door. A couple of mason jars filled with herbs crashed to the floor. The scent of something earthy, like loam in a newly plowed field, wafted upward.

"What is it?" Instinctively, his right hand went to his sidearm and he surveyed the scene outside. On Main Street, a sleek black sedan accelerated and turned out of sight from the town square.

"Are they gone?" Charlotte asked past stiff lips.

"Whoever was in that vehicle? Yes. What's this all about?"

Charlotte lifted her chin and carefully picked her way through the strewn herbs and glass shards. "Sorry, Miss Glory. I'll pay, of course. Where's your broom? I'll sweep up the mess."

Glory shooed her off, then bent over and whispered something in Charlotte's ear before addressing them both. "I'll take care of this. You go on, now, and do what you have to do."

Charlotte rummaged through the backpack and dug out a wad of bills. She lifted a hand at the sight of Glory's open mouth. "Take it. I insist. And thanks for your help."

James grabbed a jug of tea and followed Charlotte outside. He took her arm. "What really brings you to Lavender Mountain?"

Chapter Three

"Anyone ever tell you that you're stubborn as hell?" Charlotte grumbled. She climbed into James's truck, slowly swinging her injured leg into the cab, and then eased back onto the leather seat with a sigh. She wouldn't admit it for a month's salary, but running from his office had been a mistake. Her first instinct, born from years of busting street gangs and drug rings, was to flee until she'd formed a plan and was ready to strike.

James got in beside her and slammed his door shut. "Start talking."

"You're taking me back to my truck, right? I'll be out of your hair soon enough."

"That wasn't the deal. What's your game?"

She opened her mouth, and he started the engine. "Don't lie," he said. "You're not running from some ex."

She had no choice. Once he ran the gun paperwork, he'd know. "I'm an undercover cop. Atlanta PD Special Crimes Unit."

He shot her an assessing glance, then pulled the truck away from the station and into town. "What are you doing ninety miles from the big city? Anything going on around here, we should be part of the investigation. Atlanta's urban area may sprawl for miles, but this is still our jurisdiction."

He might have her cornered, but she didn't have to tell him the whole truth. "I don't suppose you'd accept the proposition that the less you know, the better?"

James snorted.

"Right. Okay, I'm investigating a missing girl and have reason to believe she's being held in the Falling Rock community."

His brow furrowed. "Why? Give me details."

"How can I be sure you're trustworthy? Well, not necessarily *you*," she amended. "But what about your boss and coworkers? Any of them could compromise—"

"I trust the sheriff explicitly," he ground out. "Harlan Sampson is as honest as they come, and I'm not saying that because he's my brother-in-law. I've known him all my life. We've been friends since third grade."

"That's fine for you, but it doesn't assure me. Far as my research shows, the previous sheriff is doing time for twenty years of covering up moonshine and murders."

"And Harlan has been working for over a year now to clean up the force," James said with a scowl.

"Are you sure he's finished? Most criminals don't work in a vacuum."

"Two officers were fired. That's out of an office with a dozen employees. I have complete faith in the ones remaining."

"But you've only worked with them six months." She'd done a cursory background search on every officer.

He shot her a glance, eyes widened in surprise. "You've done your homework," he noted, driving away from the downtown area and starting the drive up a winding mountain road.

"I know you've done a couple tours in Afghanistan. Army Special Forces."

"You seem to have me at a disadvantage," he said coolly. "I know nothing about you. Yet."

"No doubt you'll check the gun paperwork and confirm my story. I'd do the same in your position."

"So why did you break into my cabin? Couldn't you survey the Falling Rock area more directly?"

Typical cop. A rookie one, no less. "That's the difference between working undercover versus running routine patrols and answering callouts.

Direct isn't best in my line of work. I picked your cabin because it's within walking distance of where I can get a behind-the-scenes view of most of the Falling Rock houses."

"What do you expect to find? Are you hoping by some miracle that the missing girl is going to step outside? I don't foresee that happening."

Charlotte squirmed. Put that way, it did sound like a lame plan. But then, he didn't know all the particulars. He didn't know that she was investigating a ring, and as such, she hoped to observe vehicles pulling into backyards to hide the drivers' comings and goings. Even license plate numbers would provide worthwhile leads to pursue. So let him think she was foolish. The less she revealed, the less interference and lower possibility of word getting back to the traffickers that she was closing in on their operation.

"Don't make this hard," James warned. "Either voluntarily give us the information so we can help find this missing girl, or drag your feet until we force the information out of your supervisors. Your choice."

Damn it. If he contacted Atlanta, she'd be ordered—again—to stop searching. And that was the best-case scenario. Worst case, it was entirely possible she'd lose her job. But she'd weighed the risks from the start, and the decision had been easy. Jenny was her best friend's daughter. If she didn't try her best, how could she live with that knowledge? How would she be able to face her best friend for the rest of her days? She couldn't.

"If I tell you more, can we keep it between us?"

"No way. I can't keep this secret from Harlan and the others. Like you said, I'm pretty new here. Everyone else will have more experience. Don't you want the full resources the sheriff's office can provide?"

Hell, yeah. No question. Charlotte gazed out the passenger window, where shadows already lengthened with a hint of the coming twilight. To his credit, James didn't press her as she weighed the pros and cons of telling him everything. But it wasn't much of a choice, really. She had a bum leg now, and she'd been seen by the bodyguards who were obviously protecting the traffickers.

"I do need your help," she admitted. "But if you go to the sheriff, he'll contact my boss for verification of my story, and then all hell will break loose."

James's eyes narrowed. "If you're on the up-and-up, what's the problem?"

"I've been suspended." There, she'd said it. Six years of exemplary service, and now she was in the hot seat. James would think she was a total screwup.

He pulled into the cabin's driveway, shut off the engine and faced her, arms folded. "Why?"

She jerked her head from his piercing gaze and stared down at her folded hands. "Because I won't give up on this case. That's why. The official charge against me is insubordination."

"Go on," he urged at the beat of silence between them.

Charlotte lifted her head. Officer Tedder had been more than patient. He could have arrested her for trespassing, or even decided she was too much trouble and not searched for her after she'd fled. But he'd found her and coaxed her into getting help for her injury. A good man, she decided. Perhaps even a trustworthy one. She'd been burned before, but mostly, her gut and intuition had served her well in a dangerous profession.

"Can we talk somewhere other than here? Sitting in the open in your truck is an invitation for trouble." Her stomach churned as she remembered the black sedan with tinted windows that had cruised through town.

He countered with a question of his own. "Is this where you run from me again?"

"No running. You can follow me in my truck while I get a motel room, or we can go in your cabin to talk."

James drummed his fingers on the steering

wheel. "My cabin. I'll park my truck behind yours. No casual observer passing by would notice it. Probably safer than you spending the night at the local motel with your vehicle in plain view, anyway."

"Agreed."

He drove across the yard and parked behind her rental truck. Charlotte opened her door and eased onto the ground, putting most of her weight on her left leg. If it came down to another chase by land, she was doomed.

They walked across the yard, but try as she might, a low hiss of pain escaped her lips as she started up the porch steps. James placed a hand on her right forearm, and she leaned into his strength, hobbling across the wooden porch.

Damn if it wasn't heaven to feel his strong muscles taut and solid against her. For the first time since arriving at Lavender Mountain, Charlotte felt safe and protected. Not an emotional luxury she often indulged in with her line of work.

James frowned at the broken door frame as he ushered her inside. "Stay here while I check the cabin," he murmured, setting down the jug of sassafras tea from Miss Glory.

She nodded, grateful. Ordinarily that kind of take-command attitude by male coworkers annoyed her, but he was the only one around with a gun and two good legs. And he was her best hope for rescuing Jenny.

"ALL'S CLEAR," JAMES ANNOUNCED, returning to the den and placing the gun in his holster. "And I closed the back bedroom window you opened earlier this morning. You remember, the one you crawled out to run from me."

Charlotte nodded, making no apologies, and limped to the couch. Instead of collapsing into an exhausted heap, she settled in primly, back straight and feet crossed at the ankles.

What a striking woman. In the dark shadows, her hair glowed like sun fire and her eyes gleamed with intelligence, determination and... sorry to say, still a trace of wariness. Not that he blamed her for the mistrust. She'd most likely seen the worst of human nature, just as he had in Afghanistan.

He picked up the jug of tea and strode to the kitchen, where he located a glass in the near-empty cabinets. Miss Glory's tonic was purported to do wonders, and he hoped it lived up to its hype. He added ice to the glass and poured the pale, caramel-colored drink. Charlotte was being damn foolish about treating her injuries, but he couldn't force her to accept medical attention. A wry smile twitched the edges of his mouth. He imagined Charlotte Helms could be mighty stubborn when it came to changing her mind.

That was okay—he could be as damn stubborn as Charlotte, and he meant to draw out everything from her about this case. The greatest lesson he'd learned in the military was to work with others as a team. It enhanced the chance of success for any mission. He preferred a quiet, solitary life these days, but when it came to his new job, he was all about teamwork.

James returned to the den. "Drink up," he ordered, handing Charlotte the glass. "I'll be back in a minute."

"Where are you going?"

"To get my tool kit."

And his tablet, because he wasn't letting this woman out of sight again. While she slept tonight, he'd double-check her story. Insomnia came in handy every now and then.

James scanned the yard and then strode to his truck, retrieving the toolbox, the tablet, a box of crackers and a cooler packed with water bottles. Another thing the military had taught him was to be prepared. The water and crackers would satisfy their basic needs for the evening, but he longingly recalled the smell of fried chicken and mashed potatoes at the Dixie Diner. Tomorrow he'd go back and eat his fill at the lunch buffet.

Inside, Charlotte sipped tea and raised a brow. "Quite an armful. You must have been a Boy Scout."

"Lucky for you. What did Miss Glory whisper to you back at the shop?"

She blinked at the sudden question. "I couldn't understand what she muttered. Her Southern accent's pretty strong."

Again, he suspected she wasn't truthful, but in this instance, it didn't matter. Not in the grand scheme of things. He let it go. "What do you think of Miss Glory's tea?"

"Has a licorice taste. I like it. Either that, or I'm really thirsty. You believe in this stuff?"

"People who refuse standard medical treatment can hardly complain."

A surprised chuckle escaped her lips, and her eyes sparkled. "Touché."

James nearly dropped the supplies in his hand. He'd known she was attractive—that was plain to any fool—but when she smiled? Stunning.

Charlotte's eyes widened and their teal hue deepened. The space between them grew electric, humming with energy. He swallowed hard and turned away, setting down the supplies and then gripping his hammer like a lifeline. Sexual attraction was the last thing he needed in this sticky situation.

"I don't have replacement hardware, but I can nail up this door and make do for tonight. That is, if you still want to stay here?"

"You'll let me stay?" Her voice was husky, and she cleared her throat. "Thank you."

"For now. Unless your safety becomes compromised. First thing in the morning, we'll—"

"*We?* I don't need you to stay with me."

"You think I'd leave you alone out here?" He might be reluctant to get involved with people, but he always did the right thing. Or tried to. "As I was saying, at dawn, we'll get my four-wheeler, and you can show me where you were shot at."

She slowly nodded. "Like I said, I don't need your protection, but it's your cabin, after all. As far as returning to that place, it's a needle-in-a-haystack possibility, but if we can find those shell casings, it could be important down the road."

He set to work, quickly repairing the door. Satisfied, he returned to the kitchen with the cooler and put the water bottles in the fridge. The only thing edible in the refrigerator was a jar of peanut butter, and so James set the crackers and peanut butter on the table with two paper plates and a roll of paper towels.

"Dinner's served," he announced. "Basic protein and carbs."

Charlotte took a seat. "I'm used to it. If we

want to get really fancy, there are some granola bars and apples and such in my—I mean *your*—bedroom."

She started to rise, but he motioned her to stop. "I'll get them."

It wasn't fried chicken, but her contribution would add a little variety to the meal. In the bedroom, a plastic crate against the back wall was stuffed with dried foods. He lifted it, ready to carry it to the kitchen, when he spotted the laptop on her mattress. Stifling a twinge of guilt—there was a missing girl in danger, after all—he hit the space bar, hoping she hadn't properly shut it down earlier.

The screen lit and filled with images of scantily clad young girls. And by young, he noted that most didn't even appear to be sixteen years old.

"For the discerning customer," he read.

James closed the computer, lips curled in disgust. What possible connection did it have to Lavender Mountain? This was no simple kidnapping.

Charlotte's soft voice drifted down the hallway as he made his way back. "I'm doing everything I can, Tanya. I promise I won't stop until I find her." A slight pause, and then, "We'll get her back. I know it's killing you, but remember to let me call you. Not the other way around. Okay?"

As if she had eyes in the back of her head,

Charlotte spun around, cell phone at her ear, as James entered the room. "Gotta go, hon. Later."

"Sounds like this case is personal," he observed, taking a seat across from her. "Who's Tanya?"

Charlotte laid the phone down and sighed. "Why do I have the feeling you're going to pry every last detail from me?"

"Because I am," he said with a grin, spreading peanut butter on a cracker. But his amusement faded at the memory of the computer photos. "Is Tanya the mother of the missing Jenny?"

"Yes. And my best friend." Charlotte pushed away her plate. "You see why I can't quit, don't you? I mean, wouldn't you do the same for your best friend?"

He flashed back to that night in Bagram when he'd awakened in the barracks and realized the cot beside him was empty. He'd waited, figuring Steve might be in the bathroom, but the minutes had ticked by, and he knew something was wrong. Against orders, he'd sneaked out of the barracks and searched the compound until he'd found Steve—huddled behind the garbage dump, holding a gun next to his head.

It still haunted James. Another minute and his friend would have committed suicide. He'd carefully taken Steve's gun away and escorted him to the infirmary. To hell with alerting the sergeant first and following protocol for a missing soldier. He'd known in his gut that Steve was in danger. "You're not the only one with a black mark on your record," he admitted. "I understand that sometimes—"

A shot rang out.

James froze, his breathing labored. Had he imagined the sound? No, Charlotte's hands gripped the edges of the table—she'd heard it, too. This was real and in the here-and-now.

"They've found us," she whispered.

Chapter Four

Charlotte reached for her sidearm and felt nothing but bare denim at her hip. Damn. She kept forgetting James had confiscated her gun. Its absence made her feel vulnerable and powerless. First order of business in the morning was to get it back.

But that didn't help her now.

As if they'd done this together a dozen times before, she and James rose from the table and flattened their bodies against the side wall by the window.

"See anything?" she asked.

"Nothing but shadows."

"Still think it's nothing but a shot-happy hunter out there?"

"Getting a little too dark for a regular hunter," he admitted.

"As opposed to what—an irregular hunter?" she quipped. "Maybe now you'll believe me when I tell you it's Jenny's kidnappers."

James kept his gaze out the window. "Shooter's motives don't matter at the moment."

"Right. Sorry. So what's the plan?"

"We wait."

"That's it? We wait?"

"And watch."

To hell with that. "We could get on your four-wheeler and see who's out there."

"And what if that shot was meant to draw you out? You'd be a sitting duck. Stop acting like this is your first rodeo."

He was right. Damn it. This was her least favorite part of the job—stakeouts and waiting for someone else to make their next move.

"There could be more than one, you know. Maybe they're going to surround the cabin." Hugging the wall, Charlotte made her way over to the den window on the opposite side of the cabin. "I'll keep a lookout here."

Dusk settled on the woods that were wrapped in a gray mist. The outline of her rental truck at the tree line was barely visible. The vehicle was useless to her now that she suspected it had been spotted. If there was time, she'd exchange it for another one tomorrow. Her eyes and ears tingled with focus as she tried to find shifting patterns in the shadows, or the whisper of an out-of-the-ordinary snap of twigs.

"We hear another shot, call for backup," James commented.

The minutes stretched on in a tense silence, and she shifted all her weight onto her left foot.

"Knee bothering you?" he asked, his gaze still concentrated on the gathering darkness.

How did he know with his back to her? Probably a good cop to be so observant of the slightest shift in details. "Hurts a little," she admitted.

James stepped away from the window. "Let's go. If there's a stalker out there, I believe they'd have made a move by now. No sense standing around all night. We'll come back at first light and take a look around."

"Sounds like a plan." Frankly, she was relieved. Her leg hurt like hell, and there was no way she'd be able to sleep in this cabin again without worrying she'd awaken staring down the barrel of a gun.

"You stay inside while I start the truck."

"No way. We go together."

He opened his mouth to speak, but he must have read her determination. "Okay. Anything you need to bring with you?"

She'd almost forgotten. "Yeah, let me grab my stuff. I'll be quick."

Charlotte scurried to the bedroom and then stuffed her laptop in the large duffel bag already filled with clothes and toiletries, prepacked necessities in case she'd needed to leave in a hurry. She rushed back down the hall, and a chill draft from the open door blew over her body. A truck engine started outside, and headlights pierced the darkness. How dare he? But the anger was soon replaced by a seed of fear. Was he leaving her alone in this compromised location? An image of a dark alley flashed across her mind—her old partners, Roy and Danny, fading into the shadows as they ran from the drug dealer flashing his small but lethal-looking pistol. She'd run, too, but not as fast. Not near fast enough to outrun a bullet. A quick peek behind her shoulder and she saw the dealer had aimed his gun at her.

She'd turned and faced him then. Better to see the flash of gunfire and take it head-on than be hit in the back while running away.

The drug dealer unexpectedly laughed and dropped his weapon. "Some friends you got there. You ain't no coward, I give you that." His arm had lowered to his side. His features had hardened. "Get out of here," he'd growled. "And don't ever forget this is my turf."

She didn't forget. Not the dealer, nor the partners who'd left her an easy target.

Faster than she'd ever believe possible with a bum leg, Charlotte flew out of the cabin and onto the porch, duffel bag clunking across the wooden floorboards.

The truck engine rumbled in Park. James wasn't leaving without her. She climbed in the king cab, throwing the bag into the back seat, where it landed next to the gallon jug of sassafras tea he must have grabbed from the fridge.

"You tricked me," she commented. But her words held no bite.

James shifted the truck into Drive. "I don't know about the big city, but around here, we try and protect women."

"I'm a cop, not a woman."

His brow quirked.

"Well, you know what I mean."

"I'm well aware you're a woman," he said drily.

The air was charged with something other than danger this time—the space between them sparked. Charlotte cleared her dry throat. "And a cop," she insisted. "Don't forget that part."

The truck jostled along the dirt driveway. "Uh-huh, right," he muttered.

"Wait. I'm not thinking clearly." She dug into her jeans pocket for her keys. "I can drive my own truck and then exchange it for a new one in the morning. Take me back."

James pulled onto the county road. "We'll worry about your truck in the morning when we come back. For now, I think it's best we leave it."

"Okay, then. I can't argue against your logic there." Charlotte stuffed the key in her pocket.

Heat blasted from the vents, and she held her hands up against the warm air.

"Cold?" James asked.

She shrugged. "My hands are always cold."

"No gloves?"

"Somewhere in my bag. I'll dig them out later."

James opened the console and pulled out a pair of black leather gloves. "Here."

"Thanks, but that's not nec—"

"Go on. No sense suffering." He laid them in her lap.

Charlotte slipped on the overlarge gloves. They were lined with fleece and felt comfy and toasty against her skin.

The truck sped through the night, and they were in town in ten minutes. Charlotte rubbed the passenger window, scrubbing away the condensation to peer at the street. "What motel do you recommend?"

"Neither of them. There's only two."

He turned the wheel sharply, and the lights of the Dixie Diner blazed in front of her. "Why are we stopping here?" she asked.

"I'm starving. I'll pick us up a couple plates to go."

She frowned. He could have got his own meal after he dropped her off, but the rumble in her stomach couldn't argue with the need for food. Real food. Eating nothing but crackers and apples and granola bars for two days had gotten old. Charlotte followed him in, and her knees went weak at the smell of fried chicken. James ordered a meat-and-three plate for each of them, and her mouth salivated. She couldn't wait to check into her room, eat and then enjoy a long bath with no fear of intruders.

Back in the truck, James turned sideways in the seat and didn't start the motor. "This Jenny you're looking for—was she caught up in some kind of pornography ring?"

"You could say that."

"How about being a little more specific?"

It might have been framed as a question, but she knew it was a demand. Hell, if he knew this much, he might as well know the rest.

"A human trafficking ring. She's one of many girls who have been caught in its trap."

James nodded, but he didn't say a word as he started the truck and backed out of the parking space. He retraced his route and kept driving until downtown was visible only in the rearview mirror. They were far from anyone, on a lonely backroad where anything could happen.

A small frisson of fear chased down her spine. *Stop, just stop*, she chided herself. If he were one of the bad guys, he would hardly have stopped for fried chicken before doing her in. Or loaned her his gloves. Still, her hand sought the passenger door handle. "Where are we going?"

"My place."

"Now, wait a minute," she protested. "If you think—"

James held up a hand. "I have a spare bedroom. It's just a precaution."

She studied him—the hard planes of his face and his aura of calm command. Okay, she *would* feel safer staying with him. But he could have at least asked before assuming she'd follow along.

"I can't read you," she admitted. "Half the time you act like there are other explanations for the shootings, and the other half, you're extremely cautious."

"Blame my army training. I imagine all possible scenarios and then prepare for the worst."

Curiosity sparked to learn more about James. "What was it like in Afghanistan?"

His fingers drummed the dashboard as he considered his answer. "Lot of extremes. Hot during the day, cold at night. Periods of boredom followed by bursts of danger."

"I understand the boredom–danger thing. Lots of that with undercover work." Charlotte wondered if the experience had left him scarred. "What did you do in the army?"

"IED patrol."

She gave a low whistle. The man had put his life on the line with every mission. Lucky for him, he'd returned home in one piece. "Must have been tough. Do the memories ever bother you, now that you're home?" Charlotte bit her lip. This was none of her business. "Never mind. I have no right to ask. I thank you for your service."

He was silent for so long, she didn't think he was going to respond, and she stretched her right leg, trying to find a position that didn't hurt.

"It only bothers me sometimes at night," James said quietly. "Insomnia's a bitch."

JAMES SHOOK OUT two of Miss Glory's herbal pills on the kitchen table along with a glass of sassafras tea. "Drink up."

"I'm fine. My leg's not—"

"Stop it. I've seen you wince whenever you stand up or sit down. The way you favor your right leg. Are you always this stubborn?"

Charlotte picked up one of the pills and held it in her palm, frowning. "I don't like feeling out of control. Like I could fall asleep and not wake up when there's a possibility of an intruder lurking."

"Remember that insomnia I mentioned? I'll be up all night." He felt his mouth twitch. "Let my problem at least benefit you."

She bit her lip, obviously debating the wisdom of taking the pills. "What the hell." In one swift motion, she popped them in her mouth and washed them down with tea. "I don't have much faith they'll be that strong, anyway."

"Hope they work. Others swear by her herbs and roots." He knew how to make her see it his way. "Besides, get a good night's rest, and you can work longer and harder tomorrow."

"Every day Jenny spends with that ring is torture for Tanya and Jenny. I never forget that. Not for a minute."

"I don't doubt your dedication. One night's sleep will help you think clearer, and means you can bring her and the others home sooner. I saw the photos on your laptop. The ones of those girls for sale." Disgust roiled in his stomach. Hungry as he'd been, he started regretting the fried chicken and gravy.

"When did you look at my laptop? How did you—"

"When we were back at the cabin."

"Seems like I'm not the only one with a suspicious nature."

"Comes with the territory in our line of work. Never know when it might save our ass."

She shook her head, a bemused smile lighting her green-blue eyes. "Next you'll have me thanking you for doubting me."

"Good. Now let me use my influence to get

you to shower and then let me take a look at your injuries."

A tinge of red crept up her neck and face. "I can take care of myself."

"A little late for modesty. The first time we met, you weren't wearing pants."

Charlotte groaned and lifted her hands to her face. "I forgot about that."

He hadn't. Sure, at the time, he'd been a little distracted by the gun she'd aimed at him, but yeah, he'd noticed the bare, shapely legs. James rose from the table. "Go on. I'll see to cleaning up."

Charlotte rose, and again a slight wince crossed her face.

"I've got aspirin," he noted. "You don't have to strictly rely on Miss Glory's home remedies."

"Might as well give them time to work. I'll see how I feel after a bath."

Head held high, Charlotte left the kitchen, and then paused by the den's fireplace mantel. "What's this?" she asked, picking up a wooden carving of a deer and examining it closely.

"Something I whittled," he admitted, feeling self-conscious. "It's a hobby, kind of relaxing."

"This is beautiful," she murmured. "How long did it take you to make this?"

"Hard to say. I whittled on it here and there in the evenings."

"It would take me a lifetime," she said with a laugh, placing the wooden deer back on the mantel. "Besides having zero artistic talent, I'm never accused of being a patient person."

Charlotte headed to the hallway. Despite the stiff set of her back and shoulders, it was obvious that the injury bothered her.

Whether she was willing or not, if the cuts showed infection, he was taking her to a real doctor.

James stacked the paper plates and napkins, pausing at the sound of running water. Right now, Charlotte was stripping. In his house. Just down the hall. He pictured her curvy body stepping into the steamy tub and groaned. It had been way too long since he'd been with a woman.

All his nights were long, but this one might be the longest yet. Resolutely, he put up the leftover mashed potatoes and green beans. He'd get through it. He'd been through much worse.

James settled on the couch and fired up his laptop. Five minutes later, he'd confirmed that Charlotte worked for the Atlanta PD. By the time she emerged, he'd flipped on the television and attempted to watch a basketball game, but his mind was focused elsewhere.

Charlotte cleared her throat and entered the room. "This is silly, but if you must, you can see that the cuts are fine. And my knee's only a little swollen."

Her skin was damp and pink, and she tugged at the bottom of the oversize T-shirt that barely covered her underwear. James stifled his amusement. How could such a hard-ass cop be so shy?

"Come here," he said hoarsely.

She advanced to within a couple of feet and turned to the side. Slashes of jagged crimson marred the otherwise smooth, pink flesh of her leg.

James swallowed hard. "Doesn't appear to be infected. Have a seat. I'll apply some of Miss Glory's balm and put a bandage on it."

"I can do it myself."

He didn't bother arguing, just picked up the antiseptic from the coffee table and applied some to a pad of cotton. "I'll be gentle."

"You'd better be."

She sat down beside him and angled her body on her left hip, leaning her elbow on the sofa's arm. Although she hissed as he applied the antiseptic to her head wound and cuts, she didn't say a word in protest. He opened the jar of balm from Miss Glory and dabbed it on with his index finger, barely grazing the torn flesh. Quickly he put on the gauze bandage. "All done." Damn if his voice wasn't several octaves deeper.

Charlotte nodded and sat up straight. "Thank

you," she said simply. "I feel better already. I can't believe it, but those herbal pills really work." She gave a lopsided, loopy grin. "I'm getting drowsy."

He wished he could say the same. Instead, every cell in his body pulsed with energy, acutely aware of the beautiful woman who stared at him with such gratitude.

"Not too early to go to bed," he suggested.

Bed. More images played in his head of Charlotte sleeping across the hall in his guest bedroom.

She scooted sideways and lay down. "I could fall asleep right here," she murmured, wiggling her toes. Even her pink-painted toenails were adorable. As if of their own volition, his hands wrapped around her arches and he massaged her feet.

"Um, that's so nice." Her voice was husky and deep, and her eyelids fluttered.

"You must be wiped out."

"That and the pills." Her eyes widened, and she struggled to a half-seated position. Her thin T-shirt twisted, revealing a pair of lacy panties.

James reached for the afghan and covered her bare legs. A man could only take so much temptation, but he hadn't sunk so low as to take advantage of a half-drugged stranger. Hard to believe he'd known her only a day. Charlotte Helms had stormed into his life like some badass angel of justice, shaking up his quiet, orderly world.

"Do you have a girlfriend or—" her face tightened "—a wife?"

"Nope." He'd had a fiancée this time last year, but Ashley had brushed him off with a Dear John letter while he was in Afghanistan. Not that he could blame her frustration with his absence, but it rankled. Last he'd heard, she was already engaged to another man.

"What about you?" He'd assumed she wasn't married, but what did he really know about her?

She snorted. "Hell, no."

Irrational relief flowed over him.

"My profession doesn't exactly lend itself to maintaining close personal relationships," she continued. "Haven't even seen my own parents in months."

"That must be hard."

"Yeah, it's tough." Charlotte sighed and ran a hand through her long hair. "It never used to bother me, but lately…"

"Lately what?" he prompted.

"After seeing the hell Tanya's going through with her missing daughter—it kind of makes you stop and think. You shouldn't take family for granted."

"I get it. My dad and one of my sisters died last year. Made me appreciate Lilah—she's my younger sister." Lately he'd even been talking more to his estranged mother. Something he never thought he'd do after she'd run off with another man when he was in high school and had left them all high and dry.

"Lilah Tedder," she murmured, gently probing the knot by her right temple.

"She's Lilah Sampson now. Married the sheriff."

Charlotte snapped her fingers. "Thought it sounded familiar. There was a serial killer up here and—"

"Yeah, she was lucky to escape. My dad and Darla weren't so fortunate."

James shut down. He never talked about the incident. What good did it do to rehash old sorrow?

"Must have been tough," she whispered. "And then to find out the real killer was—"

"I'd rather not discuss it," he said, removing her feet from his lap and standing up.

"Of course, I understand. It's just that—"

Annoyed, James strode to the window and pushed aside an inch of curtain. A strong whipping wind battered barren treetops.

"Sorry. I'm not normally one to pry. Let's blame it on Miss Glory's herbs."

"I'm sure you read all about the case in the Atlanta papers. Heard it made the national news for a whole fifteen minutes." Even he heard the bitterness in his own voice. "Old news," he added dismissively.

Charlotte pushed aside the afghan and struggled to her feet. "How about we make some coffee? I'm good to pull my weight for a night shift. You've had a long day, too."

"Not necessary. We weren't followed. Besides, I never sleep much. No sense in you staying up, too."

"I never sleep well, either," she admitted.

He fixed his gaze on her. She'd probably witnessed a lot of the dark side of life and had her own demons, as well.

"Go on to bed. I've got this."

She yawned and cocked her head to the side. "Wake me up in about four hours?"

"Sure." He wouldn't, but he feared she'd never agree to sleep otherwise.

"Okay, then. Good night."

Charlotte started to turn, and then hesitated. Instead of leaving him, she slowly walked toward him, an uncertain gleam in her teal eyes.

She wasn't…surely, no. But she kept walking until she stood close enough that he could smell the soap from her recent bath.

"Thank you," she breathed, standing on her tiptoes.

Her lips pressed under his jaw, along the side

of his neck. Before he could react, it was over. Bemused, he watched as she left the room. It was as though her kiss had sealed his fate. He would do everything in his power to help her find the traffickers. Whether it was for Jenny and the other trapped children, or whether it was for this maddening woman—or some combination of both—James couldn't say. Indeed, such soul-searching was pointless. He'd thrown in his lot with the charismatic Charlotte.

It was going to be a long, long night.

Chapter Five

James surveyed her efforts with a critical eye. "You didn't quite get it all," he pronounced, tucking an errant lock of hair into the knitted hat. His nearness and touch made her breath hitch, although he appeared unfazed by the contact. "Don't need your flaming hair blowing in the wind like a red flag."

"Does it really matter? They're bound to hear your four-wheeler before they see anything."

"With any luck, the roar of the wind will drown out most of the noise."

Despite last night's intimacy, this morning, James was all business. Charlotte inwardly cringed, thinking of the unsolicited kiss she'd planted on him. Totally uncharacteristic of her. She recalled Miss Glory's whispered words at the shop yesterday. *"Open your heart."* Yeah, she'd understood the older woman. Probably fancied herself the local matchmaker.

James swung a long leg over the ATV and pointed to the back seat. "Hop on," he commanded.

Charlotte climbed onto it, grateful that her injuries had improved leaps and bounds overnight. Only a slight soreness remained. Once she brought Jenny home—and she would—she'd pay Miss Glory another visit and present her with a big tip.

With a lurch, James gassed the ATV, and she wrapped her arms around his waist to keep from falling. Lordy, he felt good—strong, and warm, and reliable. She resisted an impulse to bury her head against his broad back. What was it about him that drew her so? No sense falling for someone who appeared to temporarily be her partner. Emphasis on *temporarily*. She'd been burned before mixing business with pleasure. Danny had proven to be a rat bastard. Once this case was over, she'd return to Atlanta, and James Tedder would continue on with his relatively peaceful life here on Lavender Mountain. With no complications from her.

The wind was brutal in the early morning chill. Luckily James possessed more than one pair of gloves, and she'd donned the loaner ones. How cold must he be? His body shielded her from the worst of the wind.

The four-wheeler jostled and righted itself as

they drove off his cabin's property and entered the main trail leading to Falling Creek.

Finding the exact spot where she'd been shot at and searching for the left-behind shell casings wasn't likely, but they had to try. She hoped the guards were still there at the house she'd spotted, although unarmed this time. If nothing else, this morning's excursion would prove she'd told the truth about the shooting, and that there was nothing accidental about it.

Charlotte kept her eyes glued to the passing trees and brush until she spotted the clearing where she'd run off the trail. Another thirty yards or so, and they'd be in the general area. She leaned to the side. "Slow down," she called out to James. "We're close."

Close enough to also see the line of mansions on the Falling Rock bluff.

He let up on the gas and swerved off the beaten path, parking the ATV in a copse of pines, right under a handmade sign stapled to a tree. "Private Property. Trespassers will be shot on sight."

"These people are crazy," she commented, pointing to the sign.

"Yeah, you trespassed. That tends to get people shot."

She hopped off and pulled the binoculars from her backpack.

The two guards were there at the same house,

but apparently hadn't heard their approach as they conversed with one another.

"See anything?" James asked.

Charlotte pointed to the mansion in question and handed him the binoculars.

"They could be gardeners," he commented. "One's holding a rake and the other a hoe."

"Bet you could watch them an hour and you wouldn't see either of them using those tools. They're props."

"We'll keep an eye out. Where should we start looking for the casing?"

She sighed. "Here's as good a spot as any."

They separated and began combing the grounds. Charlotte hugged her arms to her waist, eyes focused on finding the small object amid the dead leaves and brown twigs. You'd think it would stand out, but they were hampered by being unable to pinpoint the exact location of the shooting. Too bad she hadn't thought to leave some sort of mark behind. That way, they could estimate how far away the shooter was when he fired his weapon.

"Found one," James called.

"Really? Damn, you must have eagle eyes." She scurried over.

James held it up to the sun, squinting at it a moment before dropping the casing into a small plastic baggie.

"What now?" she asked through chattering teeth. "Keep watching the guards?" She lifted her binoculars. They were still talking, gesturing broadly with their hands, the garden implements dangling uselessly by their sides. The men started pushing and shoving. "We're in luck today. They're too busy fighting each other to notice us."

"Then let's push it. We'll ride down the trail—it turns and runs perpendicular to the houses."

"What if they see us?"

He shrugged. "They'll just think we're out on a joyride."

"In this weather?" she asked skeptically.

"I want to gauge their reaction for myself."

Some small part of him still had reservations about her story. "You're the one sitting in front. If they shoot—"

"Exactly." James stuffed the baggie in his coat pocket and climbed on the ATV.

Charlotte lifted the binoculars one last time. The guards were throwing actual punches. Good to know the idiot thugs were so easily distracted. She tilted the binoculars upward, scanning the windows.

A face appeared. A young girl with long blond hair, nose almost pressed to the windowpane. The look of misery and longing in her blue eyes punched Charlotte in the gut. "I see a possible victim," she whispered, the sound of her voice lost in the wind.

"What's that?" James asked, immediately by her side. "Let me see."

She passed him the binoculars and hurriedly dug into her backpack for the camera. "Top left window."

James peered through the lens. "I don't see anything."

"Give it here." Charlotte dropped the camera, grabbed the field glasses, and pinpointed the target.

Nothing. The blinds were drawn closed. She hadn't imagined it—Jenny had been there seconds ago. "Damn it! Jenny was just there. I promise you."

"Too bad. If she'd stayed thirty seconds longer, you could have snapped a photo. Would have been solid proof to justify a search warrant of the house."

"I know," she said with a groan. "Who knows when or if she'll appear again?"

He laid a warm, heavy hand on her shoulder and gave it a quick squeeze. "At least we know where to focus our efforts now if that particular household doesn't claim children."

Our efforts. The world went bleary through a thick haze of tears, and Charlotte angrily blinked them back. She cleared her throat. "Does this mean you believe me? You'll help bring those bastards down?"

James stared ahead. "I saw the pictures of those missing children." A muscle worked in his jaw. "If they're being held there—" he nodded at the house "—then I'll stop at nothing to get them out."

Something tight in her shoulders relaxed slightly—a tension she hadn't been aware she was carrying. "That's where they are. I know for sure now, even if I can't prove it to anyone else."

Again she felt for the missing gun at her side. Maybe it was a good thing that James had confiscated it. She wanted nothing more than to force her way inside and search the premises. But even armed, it would take more than one person to get the captives out alive. *Soon*, she silently promised Jenny.

"Let's take 'er for a spin," James said, hopping on the ATV.

Privately she was unconvinced of the wisdom of that particular move, but partnerships were a give-and-take. She'd voiced her concern, and he'd overridden it. Fair enough. He'd been accommodating in other matters.

Charlotte resumed her position on the back seat, and they blazed down the trail. At last they were close enough to the guards that the men must have heard the oncoming vehicle. They pulled apart, warily eying their approach. Both drew their right hands to their hips as if reaching for sidearms.

SURELY THEY WEREN'T so brazen as to shoot two people in broad daylight.

But perhaps he'd been a fool to count on that. He couldn't let anything happen to Charlotte. Coming out here had been his idea. James threw up his right hand in a friendly wave, as if he were merely passing through without a care in the world.

They didn't return the wave or the smile, but they didn't fire, either.

James turned to the left and followed the path that led away from the territory the men guarded. Might be best not to return the same way, just to be safe. Another half mile ahead, he could cut across Old Man Broward's field and return to the cabin in a more roundabout fashion.

Charlotte tugged violently on his right arm. "Stop!"

Had they been followed? James veered the ATV sideways, slamming on the brakes. His eyes cut to the path behind them. "What is it?"

Before the ATV completely sputtered to a stop,

Charlotte hopped off and rushed to the side of the road, pointing. "Is that blood?"

Dark crimson dotted and swiped across dried leaves.

"The drag pattern indicates something was shot and dragged here," he mused.

"Or *someone*," Charlotte said, rubbing her arms. "Oh, God, I hope it's not Jenny. Not that I want anyone dead, of course. It's just, I couldn't ear for Tanya to lose her only child. Her marriage went south last year, and Jenny is her world."

"Every girl is somebody's daughter. Somebody's world, too. But I know what you mean."

He dug another plastic bag from his coat pocket and bent down to collect a sample. "An eventful morning," he said grimly.

"Wait. Let me take a photo of this before you start collecting."

He waited, studying the blood. No way to tell if it was animal or human without running tests. There was a lot of it. If it was from a human, chances were they were dead. The body—or possibly a deer carcass—had been dragged a couple of feet before being hauled off.

A few snaps and clicks later, James quickly gathered up enough blood for lab testing and then drove the meandering route back to the cabin.

During the truck ride to the sheriff's department, Charlotte was unusually quiet and withdrawn. James took her hand. "We're going to free Jenny and the others," he promised, parking the truck.

She squeezed his hand, and he withdrew it. James stepped out of the vehicle, and she fell into place beside him as they entered the sheriff's office. Why did he always feel the need to touch Charlotte? Totally inappropriate and nothing he'd ever felt the urge to do on the few patrols he'd run with Jolene, the only female officer in the department. Must be because this case was personal for Charlotte and she was passionate about freeing the prisoners. She cared deeply about this assignment.

Hell, so did he. Hard to believe in America, and right here in his county, young girls were brutalized and sold to men like sides of beef. Made it damn hard to sleep at night, imagining their suffering.

The clatter and whir of printers and scanners abruptly stopped. Necks craned, and fingers stilled over keyboards. For a good five seconds, he and Charlotte were scrutinized by Elmore County's finest.

Sammy arose from his desk and walked over to greet them. "Wondered where you were this morning," he remarked. He extended a hand to Charlotte. "Sam Armstrong."

"Detective Helms." She gave a polite nod

but volunteered nothing further about herself. Sammy turned back to James. "You're late this morning. Boss wants to see you. Pronto."

That sounded fairly ominous. As the newest officer, he had no authority deciding what cases to take, much less setting his own schedule.

"Shall I go with you?" Charlotte asked, squaring her shoulders.

"Later. Let me talk to him first." He'd sent Harlan a couple of brief texts stating only that he was investigating a trafficking ring with an Atlanta cop. No doubt Harlan was less than pleased at being left out.

"How about some coffee?" Sammy asked, steering Charlotte toward the back of the lobby.

"Sure. Just point me in the right direction."

Once she walked a few feet away, Sammy leaned in, amusement flickering in his eyes. "Want me to handcuff her to the desk this time? She appears to be a flight risk."

"You can try, but I have a suspicion you'd end up the one chained to my desk. Not Charlotte."

Sammy laughed. "I like her spirit."

"Guess I better go face the music with Harlan."

"He's in a rotten mood this morning," Sammy cheerily informed him.

James stifled a groan and strode the hallway

to Harlan's office. The sheriff sat at his desk, a newspaper sprawled out in front of him.

"Sir?" James asked, always formal in the workplace. He didn't want Harlan or anyone else to think he courted favor because the sheriff was his brother-in-law.

Harlan scowled, impatiently waving for him to take a seat. "Cut the *sir* crap. You aren't in the army anymore."

A fact James never intended to use to his advantage. "Yes, s—"

"Call me Harlan like everybody else around here." He leaned back in his chair, steepling his fingers. "What the hell is this about a human trafficking ring, and who's working undercover in my county?"

"Yesterday I found a woman camped out in Dad's old cabin. Turns out she's an undercover cop with Atlanta's special crimes unit. Her name's Detective Helms." He tried not to grimace as Harlan punched her name into his computer.

"Might as well tell you," James said. "Char—Detective Helms—is currently on suspension with them for insubordination."

Harlan stopped typing and cast him a surprised scowl. "Why?"

"She was ordered to drop her search and was reassigned another case. She refused."

"Why?" Harlan barked again. It seemed to be his favorite word.

"Because one of the victims is the daughter of her best friend."

"An officer can't allow personal emotions to interfere with duty," Harlan objected. "If she was ordered to cease, then that's the end of the matter."

James quirked a brow. "Like you did when J.D. ordered you to mind your own business last year when Lilah was in danger?"

What an ass the former sheriff had been. He'd never cared for the guy and wasn't a bit surprised when he returned home and learned J.D. was in jail. Especially since he'd protected the identity of James's father and sister's killer. Mentally James shook off the memory of his own tragedy.

Harlan shifted in his seat. "If I had stopped my investigation, your sister might have been the next victim."

"I'm not complaining, merely pointing out that sometimes it's impossible to give up."

It was easy to read Harlan's discomfort as his boss realized the hypocrisy of the situation. James went in for the kill.

"What harm can it be to work with her for a time? Worst-case scenario, it's been a waste of one officer's time. Best case, we find the traffickers, and you get all the glory for the capture."

"You really think that's all I care about? What people will think of me?"

He'd overstepped his bounds. Of course Harlan cared how all this would reflect on him as sheriff. It was an elected position, after all. But he was also a decent man intent on keeping crime out of the county.

"I was out of line," James admitted. "But I know you. If young girls are being held against their will and sold into the sex slave market, you'll do your best to stop it."

"Damn right," Harlan grumbled.

"So you'll let me continue working the case with Detective Helms?"

Harlan regarded him silently for several heartbeats. "With reservations. I'm going to speak with her supervisor and get more information on this suspension. In the meantime, tell me what, if anything, you've discovered that validates her claim of a ring operating out of Lavender Mountain."

Quickly he filled Harlan in on the attempted shooting, being tailed by an unmarked sedan, the shot in the dark last night and Charlotte's claim of seeing a young girl's face at the window this morning. "And then there's this," he added, pulling out the baggie of bloody leaves. "Found them close to the Falling Rock subdivision."

Harlan leaned over his desk and picked up the

evidence, holding it up to the light. "Could be from a deer."

"Or it could be human."

Harlan nodded. "I'll send it to the lab straight-away and pull strings. They should know in a day or two if it's animal or human, but the DNA tests to determine whose blood it is could take weeks. And even then, we can only match DNA if the person has a DNA sample on file."

Then he drummed his fingers against the wooden desk. "So far, you haven't proven anything sinister is going on at Falling Rock, but I don't want to take chances, either. I'll get the lowdown on this Helms woman, but in the meantime, check out her story." Harlan narrowed his eyes. "Heard she's a real looker. You aren't getting sucked in by a pretty face, are you?"

"'Course not." James swallowed back his irritation. "She's sacrificing everything to rescue her friend's daughter and whoever else is held captive."

Harlan let out a sigh. "So she claims. How long does she plan on staying?"

"As long as it takes."

"And where's she staying?"

Heat blossomed on his neck and face. "I've offered her my place." That sounded bad. Really bad. But he hated the idea of Charlotte staying in town and being exposed to danger.

Thankfully Harlan let that pass. "Suspension or not, Atlanta should have informed me of suspicious activity in this area. We've got enough problems without being in the dark on any leads they have. It's an insult to this office. An insult to me."

"Don't take it personally. It's the nature of undercover work. And Elmore County's reputation is ruined after all the crap J.D. pulled as sheriff."

Harlan didn't appear the least mollified. "They're still going to hear my complaint. Are you still sure this Helms woman is on the up-and-up?"

James immediately leaped to her defense. "Yes. A bit reckless, but brave and determined."

"Reckless?" asked a high-pitched voice.

Charlotte stood in the doorway, arms folded and chin lifted. "Nothing's ever been accomplished without taking action based on calculated risks."

Harlan stood and assessed her with narrow eyes. "I don't want my officer placed at risk with any wild plans you might harbor for accomplishing your mission. Got it? Any evidence you find, you run it by me, and I'll decide what action to take."

"Got it." Her lips tightened to a thin line, and James was willing to bet she told Harlan only what he wanted to hear. Obedience didn't appear to be her strong suit.

"Excellent," Harlan said crisply. "As long as we have that understanding, Officer Tedder can work with you a few days to see if you two can turn up evidence. We'll issue you a uniform and a cover story that you're our new employee on probation and learning the ropes. Not being undercover will allow you to freely explore the area. That sound fair?"

"Perfectly."

Harlan buzzed the intercom on his desk and his secretary, Zelda, appeared immediately. "Escort Detective Helms to inventory and see she's issued a suitable uniform," he told her. "If there's not one in her size, check around with a few of the neighboring sheriffs and see if they have a spare."

"I'm on it."

Zelda motioned for Charlotte to follow, and James was alone again with his boss.

"I appreciate this," James began. "I realize I'm still fairly new, and if it turns out—"

"We're already understaffed, and all my other officers have a huge workload as it is." Harlan relaxed and sat back down. "Besides, I wouldn't have hired you if I didn't think you were up for the job, and any assignment, brother-in-law or not."

James had his doubts about that. Lilah had

fussed over him ever since he'd returned from Afghanistan, convinced he needed to get out of the house more. No one seemed to understand that after all he'd seen overseas, living alone and keeping to himself was his idea of paradise. He wanted nothing more than peace and quiet, but he suspected that ship had sailed.

The phone rang, and Harlan glanced at the screen. "Got to take this. Keep me informed. And James...keep your guard up, okay?"

With that, Harlan lifted the phone's handset, and James returned to his desk, mulling over the conversation. His feelings were mixed. It *was* an interesting case and one he'd campaigned to stay on. One that beat the hell out of roaming the back roads on patrol. But Charlotte unsettled him. He couldn't stop thinking about her haunted eyes when she mentioned Jenny. The need to leap to her defense had been surprising—and not in a good way.

Was he being fooled by a pretty face, as Harlan suggested?

He'd take his brother-in-law's warning to heart. Proceed slow and easy. And for God's sake, he'd resist the impulse to touch her. Detective Charlotte Helms was temporarily his new partner—and nothing more.

Chapter Six

"May I have my gun back now—partner?" Charlotte self-consciously tugged at the front of her too-tight uniform blouse. First opportunity, she'd buy some dark brown tank tops to wear underneath the shirt. Pink skin on her chest and stomach peeked out in the gap between the buttons. She was a quarter-pound cheeseburger away from completely popping out.

James's eyes slid down her uniform, and she barely resisted the urge to squirm. The pants were as tight as the top, hugging her hips and ass in a way that made her feel exposed.

"Right. Your gun." He unlocked a desk drawer. "Zelda's made arrangements for better-fitting uniforms to be overnighted."

Was it her imagination, or had his voice deepened and slowed? Suddenly it wasn't just her uniform that felt tight. The very room felt compressed and the air thick with tension.

Sexual tension.

Might as well call it what it was. Charlotte swallowed hard, eyes focused on his large hands as they palmed her weapon—metal caressed by muscle. Mesmerizing. What would it be like to have his hands stroke her naked flesh?

"Here," James said, his hand reaching for hers.

Lifting her arm was like a magnetic pull through molasses—slow and steady and inevitable. Her fingers wrapped around the gun's barrel, and she fastened it to her belt clip. She didn't dare face James. Didn't dare trust her eyes not to betray the sudden passion.

"Thank you," she murmured. Damn if her voice wasn't as gruff as his.

Buck up. He's officially your partner now. Passion meant distraction. And they each needed all their wits to break the trafficking ring. Not to mention, they also needed focus to keep their hides intact in the face of flying bullets. No wonder romantic relationships were taboo in law enforcement—they could get you killed. And once you broke up with a coworker? The worst. Danny had taught her that.

"For you."

Her eyes snapped to the doorway as Sam entered the room waving a thick manila envelope, which he tossed in James's inbox. His forehead crinkled. "Something going on in here?"

"No, thanks for—" James began.

"Nope," she denied.

He glanced between them, realization dawning in his eyes. "Right. Whatever you say."

Charlotte rummaged through her backpack for her case files, ignoring Sam as he swept out of the room. The situation was awkward enough without the man's teasing. She cleared her throat and spread her files across his desk. "Let's get down to it, shall we? Here's a photo of Jenny."

The blown-up color print portrayed a smiling girl, her mother's arm slung across her shoulder. The girl's eyes and skin had that glow that came only with youth. Tanya's grin was carefree and proud—in contrast to the past two weeks, when her eyes had been practically swollen shut from crying and her face puffy with misery. As thankful as Tanya would be when her daughter returned home—and Charlotte vowed to make it so—she suspected that Tanya's carefree look was gone forever.

"Jenny Ashbury," she said softly. "I also have photos of other missing girls ages twelve to sixteen, although most are twelve to fourteen years old. We tried a sting operation using me as bait, but I only drew men wanting to hire me as a prostitute. I'm too old to be considered a prime target for trafficking."

"Too old?" James shook his head in disgust and looked over the mug shots.

"Anyone look familiar?" she asked.

"No."

"Well, that was a long shot, but it could be helpful if you familiarized yourself with their faces and names. Never know when they might slip up and one of the girls escapes."

"Will do. I'm printing out the owner names and information for all the houses at Falling Rock. In the meantime, fill me in on everything you have."

Charlotte settled into a seat. "We've known for some time that a woman is locating and luring vulnerable young girls—runaways, foster children, the homeless, you get the picture. We don't know her name, but our nickname for her is Piper, short for Pied Piper."

"Where are you getting your info?"

"Mostly from Karen Hicks, a thirteen-year-old runaway who managed to escape. Piper befriended her after discovering her roaming around on Peachtree Street. Bought her a meal and offered to put her up for a night at a motel."

James frowned. "Your Piper's a class act. But I don't see the connection. Lavender Mountain's a long way from downtown Atlanta."

Charlotte couldn't mask her distaste. "According to Karen, two armed men forced her and three other girls into a van, bound and blindfolded them, then drove them around for a couple of hours. They were offloaded at a huge, luxurious house…and then they spent the next week being instructed in the finer points of sexual relations."

"Lovely," James muttered.

"Oh, it gets better. Karen found out that there was to be a party that weekend where Piper's clients could come and sample the goods. If they liked what they found, the girls were to be sold at a price—either as exclusive property to their new owner, or to a man who would pimp them out to others."

Charlotte shook her head. Poor Karen. At first glimpse, her prison must have seemed like a fairy-tale castle. But it hadn't taken long for the illusion to shatter—there would be no happily-ever-after on the horizon.

"How did she manage to escape?"

"Luckily for Karen, one of the rapists who visited there was not only excited but also stupid. He forgot to lock them up from the outside of the bedroom door before he asked her to tie him up and gag him. Karen happily complied, managed to slip out the back door, and then hitched rides back to Atlanta."

James tapped an index finger to his lips, a thoughtful expression in his eyes. "And Karen claims this happened at Falling Rock?"

"When she escaped, she noticed the entrance

sign on the subdivision gate. Unfortunately, she never got the house address. She and the others were kept in the basement, and once she got free, she didn't stop running to look back."

"What about a description of the captors?"

"Middle-aged white couple of medium build. Man had gray hair and woman had brown hair. Both blue-eyed. In other words, generic."

"We can show Karen photos of the different property owners and have her identify which couple held—"

"Karen's long gone. I can only assume she's left the Atlanta area. No family or friends have heard from her in weeks." Charlotte feared the worst for her former informant.

James pulled the plat map of Falling Rock from the printer and circled one property in red. "Pretty sure this is the house we observed with the gardeners out back and where you saw the girl at the window. It belongs to Richard and Madeline Stowers, who have no children. We're in luck."

Her heartbeat quickened. "Why? Do you know them?"

"Barely. Not like we run in the same social circles. But next week, they're hosting the annual fund-raiser for the sheriff's office." He gave a grim smile. "And we're always invited to attend. Every officer—including new trainees."

Charlotte slapped her hands on the desk and grinned. Finally, an opportunity to access the grounds. "Bam. We can take advantage of that and sneak around." But as suddenly as elation surged through her body, it deflated. "Still, a whole week...they'll have moved the girls out by then. Sure, it's brazen enough that they're holding y'all a fund-raiser, but to keep the girls locked up for hours with a dozen lawmen in the same house? I don't see it happening."

"Oh, the fund-raiser won't be at their house. They hold it at the Falling Rock Community Clubhouse." He pointed to the map. "The clubhouse is only three doors down from the Stowerses' cabin, though. They plan on trying to sell the girls practically right under our noses."

"Perfect cover," she pointed out. "Invite all the law enforcement officers to the ball—which leaves no one patrolling the streets." Charlotte stood, restless and hungry with the need for action. "I want to see their home and the clubhouse from the front. I couldn't do a safe drive-by in my rental, but what if we took a patrol car for a spin? We'd be providing a routine public service, right?"

"I'm all in." He pushed back his chair and grabbed his jacket. "Don't forget your camera. With any luck, you'll catch a glimpse of Jenny."

JAMES KEPT HIS gaze fixed on the winding mountain road. Something had happened back there in the office—unspoken, unexpected and unwanted. Sure, there had been a few flashes of heat before, but now their chemistry crackled and burned with tension. Charlotte's presence filled the vehicle, filled his mind and filled his senses.

"Fancy, shmancy," she commented as the Falling Rock entrance came into view. By the gatehouse was a large stone wall with a six-foot waterfall feature.

"Only the best for these folks." Despite all his years away and his overseas stints, James's nerves were still set on edge whenever he crossed into the exclusive community. Growing up as the son of a local moonshiner hadn't been easy. Even by Lavender Mountain standards, his family had been poor and looked down upon. In many ways, the situation was even worse since the Tedder name had been linked to a string of murders last year. The disparity between the rich and poor couldn't be more evident.

Charlotte's voice wrenched him out of his thoughts. "Do they keep this gate manned 24/7?"

"Yep. The guards are paid out of homeowner association fees. Must pay them fairly well, too—there's seldom any turnover. Then again," he admitted, "steady jobs are hard to come by around here."

"Could be the Stowerses pay them a little something extra to turn a blind eye to their comings and goings," she mused.

James pulled up to the gate and rolled down his window. Les Phelps leaned out the gatehouse window with a clipboard. "Afternoon, Officer Tedder. Cold day today."

"Hey, Les. Meet our new officer, Bailey Hanson. I'm showing her around the area. Letting her get a feel for the lay of the land."

His gaunt face lit on Charlotte with interest. "Howdy, ma'am. Pleasure to meet ya."

Charlotte leaned forward and gave a friendly wave. "You write down every vehicle that comes and goes here?"

"Yes, ma'am. Make, model, time of arrival and time of departure. Always take a quick glance at strangers' driver's licenses, too. All day, every day."

"Bet nothing gets by you," she said with a coy smile.

"No, ma'am. It surely don't." He blushed and continued staring at Charlotte. "I take my job seriously."

"I don't doubt it for a minute." Her voice practically purred.

Irritation spiked James's blood pressure. Charlotte never spoke to *him* that way. "Thanks, Les," he muttered, then rolled up the window and hit the gas pedal.

Charlotte eased back into her seat. "How well do you know that guy?"

"I've seen him around. He was a couple grades behind me in school."

"Trustworthy or no?"

"Never been in trouble with the law, as far as I know. Seemed an okay kid."

"Not exactly a ringing endorsement."

He shrugged. "How can you ever really know what goes on in other people's lives? We all wear a mask to some degree. For all I know, Les might be a serial killer."

And he wasn't being flippant. Even family members sometimes weren't what they seemed— as he well knew.

Charlotte snorted. "And here I thought *I* was jaded. You're just as bad."

The road climbed until they rounded a bend and faced the first behemoth of stone and wood and glass. Charlotte gave an appreciative whistle. "Sweet little mansions you've got here. I bet most of the owners don't even live here full-time."

"Most don't," he agreed. "We hardly ever see them during the cold months unless it's for the fund-raiser or a holiday." James slowed the car.

"And here we are. Third house on the left belongs to the Stowerses."

"Nice digs," she commented, studying the house. "Would it be possible to get an architect's drawing of the floorplan? Could come in handy later."

"I'll check. Shouldn't be a problem since the architect lives in Falling Rock. He'll want to help keep his community safe and clean."

"I take it there's only one entrance to Falling Rock?"

"It's the only paved road, yes."

"Good point. I noticed the jeep and four-wheeler trails along the back of the properties on this side of the street. We'll need a lookout posted front and back to secure the neighborhood."

"Harlan would agree to the needed manpower if we could show some proof that the girls are trapped there."

"Proof?" Charlotte slapped the dashboard and huffed, "She's there. It's so frustrating trying to prove it."

"You're a cop. You know how this works."

"I know," she muttered, staring at the dashboard. "I'm just... I call Tanya every night and have to give her bad news."

"But tonight you'll have good news. You saw Jenny. As long as she's alive, there's hope."

She sighed and rubbed her temples. "You're

right. I can't imagine what it's like for Tanya, though."

He didn't want to do it, damn it, but he couldn't resist. Couldn't bear to see the misery in her eyes. James reached across the console and took her hand. Her fingers encircled his and held on. They didn't speak as they left Falling Rock and traveled back down Blood Mountain.

Peace settled over James. It was inappropriate, ill-advised and one step closer to heartbreak. Charlotte was his partner—a temporary one, at that. Once this case was over, she'd return to her life in Atlanta and forget all about him, just as Ashley had forgotten him while he was in Afghanistan.

And yet he held on to her hand.

A black car slowly exited Falling Rock and fell into place behind their vehicle. Although darkness had not yet fallen, it was impossible to make out the driver through the tinted windows. Reluctantly James removed his hand from Charlotte's and placed it on the steering wheel.

She instantly sensed trouble. "What is it?"

"Black sedan behind us. Just keeping an eye out since you were followed by one in town."

She straightened in her seat and turned her neck. "Holy," she grunted. "I'm glad I have a gun this time. And you beside me."

The five-mile stretch between them and town

was practically deserted. A growing unease prickled his scalp as the sedan picked up speed and drew closer. Close enough that if he came to a sudden stop, the vehicle would ram into theirs. Two men were in that car, but he couldn't make out their individual features. James hit the accelerator.

The sedan did the same. An arm emerged from its passenger-side window, and a gun took aim.

"Get down!" he shouted, and shoved Charlotte's head below the glass. "They've got a—"

The ping of gunfire erupted, followed immediately by the grate of metal against metal as a bullet connected with fender.

His mind cleared and narrowed to a crystallized focus. He had to get them to safety. His brain worked at warp speed, calculating his options. It was another four miles to town, and he was willing to bet that the snipers wouldn't shoot with eyewitnesses around. And he knew every hairpin twist on this road—advantage, him. So…his best bet was to drive fast and weave the cruiser so that the snipers would have a more difficult shot.

Charlotte turned on the walkie-talkie. "Come in. This is Officer Hanson. We're at mile marker three on County Road 143. Officers needs help. Shots fired. All available backup needed *immediately.*"

James rounded a curve and jerked the steering

wheel to the left. Another bullet fired, missing them completely. Quickly he maneuvered back into the right lane. Paved road and faded lines of white paint rose to greet him at a dizzying speed.

Ping. Glass shards exploded from the back window. He slowed for an instant, ensuring Charlotte was unharmed.

"That's it, damn it!" Charlotte loaded her gun, unrolled the passenger window, and halfway leaned out.

"What are you—"

The roar of her shot exploded, and James tugged at her jacket. "Get down!"

"No way." She took aim and fired again. "Missed. At least they're slowing."

"How the hell am I supposed to drive? One sharp turn and your ass will fall out that window."

"Don't worry about me. You focus on the road."

James gritted his teeth. If they managed to survive the next five minutes, Charlotte was in for a tongue lashing of a magnitude she'd never experienced. He was the lead, and as such, he had the right to—

A red pickup truck swerved around the corner, and James jerked the car back into his own lane. Only inches of space separated their vehicles. There was barely time to register the man's shocked face, and then he heard him lay on his horn. No doubt Harlan would be getting a civilian complaint about his reckless driving. So be it.

Another mile and a half passed. A few sprinklings of barns and cabins dotted the wintry landscape. They were getting closer to safety.

Charlotte fired again. "Got 'em! Bullet went through their windshield, but I'm not sure if it hit one of them."

And her tone indicated she hoped that the bullet found its human mark. A surge of admiration, mixed with adrenaline, rushed through him. He'd take Charlotte Helms as a partner any day, every day.

His bubble of appreciation burst as their cruiser suddenly pitched to the left. The sniper had shot out his left rear tire. James fought to keep the cruiser from veering over the side of the mountain. The flimsy guardrails would never hold back over three tons of speeding metal. Soon the heat from the tire rim grinding on pavement might lock up his brakes.

And that would be it. They'd come to a dead halt and be a sitting target. Orange and red sparks tunneled upward from the rear of the cruiser.

From a distance, the whirring of sirens approached. Would it be too late?

The sedan surged forward, trying to pass him

on the left. Its right front fender crashed into them, and the cruiser spun out of control.

Round and round they flew in a circus ride of terror. He caught glimpses of Charlotte's face, which was set, grim and determined, even if her voice shook. "I'm ready to face them," she declared, one hand on the dashboard to keep from flying about, the other gripping her weapon.

The cruiser slowed its spin, and James withdrew his gun. This was it.

Another burst of gunfire erupted from beside him. "I hit their front tire," Charlotte said. "Take *that*, you bastards!"

The sedan took a sudden dive to the right, flipping over the guardrail like dandelion seeds in the wind. James slammed on the brakes, abandoned his vehicle and rushed to the rail, Charlotte one step ahead of him.

On and on it rolled. "Radio for an ambulance," he said.

"I'm going down." Charlotte hopped over the mangled guardrail and slowly walked down the steep incline, holstering her weapon.

"What the hell," he muttered. Backup was on the way. It was more important that he stay close to Charlotte. Bastards were like cats—they always seemed to have nine lives. No way would he risk letting one of them shoot at her. And she still favored her right leg after yesterday's flesh wound.

"Careful," he warned. "They might still be alive and dangerous."

"As if this is my first day as a cop," she muttered as she continued the slow descent. Rocks and roots marred the surface, and bits of gravel tumbled beneath his feet.

Oomph. Charlotte went down, feet flying out from under her, and tumbled a good ten feet on her side. James stumbled and slid to a halt beside her. "You okay?"

"Hell, no." Her breathing was jagged and raspy, her forehead scratched and bleeding. "My side hurts."

No blood that he could observe. Gently he ran a hand down her left rib cage. "Here?"

Charlotte moaned and batted his hand away.

"Probably cracked ribs," he said. "And maybe even internal injury."

"Who cares? Just go. Don't let those guys get away."

"You sure?"

She waved a hand. "Go!"

The siren wails grew louder—the cavalry would arrive soon enough.

"I'll send the backup your way," she urged.

He nodded and scrambled down the incline. Two men dressed in black pants and navy T-shirts crawled out of the sedan. One ran for the tree line, cradling his arm, and the other tried to run, but clutched his right leg and limped along at a slower clip.

James picked up his pace, half sliding and half jogging downward. What rotten luck that a tree hadn't broken the sedan's fall. Instead, it had rolled to a stop twenty yards from the edge of the woods. Gray smoke from its engine spiraled upward. Damn, the sedan could go up in flames at any moment.

The smell of leaking fuel brought him to a standstill. A whoosh of dizziness descended and he was again sucked into that quicksand of a flashback. A merciless sun beat down on the top of his head and his skin gritted and stung from an Afghan sandstorm. The enemy jeep approached and he was powerless to escape. Brain, body and lungs tightened into paralysis. He couldn't move or think past the boa-constricting fear that wrapped around his chest and squeezed and squeezed and squeezed.

"Look out!" Charlotte called, the words barely audible in the heavy gusts. But her voice cut through the time and distance his mind had created. The constriction in his chest loosened and he ran to the side of the smoking sedan, keeping plenty of distance between the smoking vehicle and himself. A curl of fire arose, licking the engine.

He ran as fast as he could, yet when the sedan exploded, the heat from the conflagration scorched his body like a blast furnace. How long had he been standing there, body present but his mind a thousand miles away? Probably enough time for the men to escape. They were nowhere in sight. He couldn't let them disappear and perhaps ruin their best chance of cracking the ring.

He ran into the woods, the brightness of the day dropping away. James withdrew his gun, stepped behind a tree, and surveyed the area. The men could be standing behind one of the wider oaks or curled down behind dense shrubbery and foliage. "Drop your weapons and give yourselves up!" he shouted.

The wind whistled and tree limbs rattled, but no other sounds emerged. How far had they managed to run?

At the distant shouts from behind him, James turned to find several officers making a slow descent down the mountain. Once more backup arrived, they could all spread out and search the area, but the sinking despair in his stomach said it would be fruitless. He knew only too well that it was easy for a man to hide out in these parts. The land was wild and tangled, populated with caves and plenty of nooks and crannies for desperate—or lucky—fugitives.

Damn it to hell. When were they going to catch a break in this case?

Chapter Seven

A helicopter roared overhead in the almost black sky, making conversation difficult. Harlan gestured for James and Charlotte to follow him to his cruiser. Inside, James took the back seat with Charlotte while Harlan started the engine and cranked up the heater. He took off his gloves and warmed his hands over the vent.

"Sure you don't want to go to the hospital and have your injuries looked at?" he asked, spinning around and addressing Charlotte.

"For the last time, *no*. All I've got is a scratch on the forehead and some bruised ribs."

Despite his misery of self-disgust over the PTSD issues, James's lips quirked upward. The woman obviously had a thing against doctors.

"No point in you both hanging around all night," Harlan said. "I'm keeping an officer on patrol at Falling Rock in case the men return there on foot. And I'm sending the rest of the search party home, helicopter included. I'll deploy men again at first light. For now, we've done all we can do."

James ran a hand through his close-cropped hair. "How about we question Les one more time—"

"Forget it. He's told us all he knows. Thanks to him, we have the sedan's tag number, at least."

"For all the good that did," Charlotte grumbled.

Another dead end in the case. The sedan was rented from an Atlanta company, but the driver had provided a fake ID. Shame lanced through him yet again. That damn PTSD. So far, Charlotte hadn't brought up today's failure, but he couldn't let it go.

"More bad news," Harlan continued. "Sammy got ahold of the Stowerses. He and his wife are still in Atlanta, and he claims no knowledge of who the men could be. I tend to believe him. Listen, y'all go ahead and crash for the evening. You've had enough excitement for one day. And you're bound to be bruised and sore come morning."

James was fine and wound-up enough to work all night, to make up for his lapse. But despite her bravado, Charlotte's eyes sported half moons of dark shadows, and she kept rubbing her temples as if trying to ward off a headache.

"I agree." Charlotte's mouth opened to object, and James sped up to stop her argument. "The best course is for us to get a good night's sleep and start fresh in the morning." He ached to reach an arm around Charlotte, but if Harlan saw the attraction between them, he'd more than likely assign another officer to work with her.

James wasn't about to let that happen.

Harlan nodded approval and pulled out onto the road. "I'll give you a lift home. Come to the station as soon as you're able in the morning, and we'll work out a plan of attack."

They left behind the strobing blue lights of a dozen cop cars and entered the thick blackness of unlit country roads. In the crystal coldness, the stars and moon were lit like a jeweled candelabra. At the edge of town, Harlan pulled into James's driveway. A familiar red car was parked outside, and the lights inside were on.

"Lilah's here," Harlan explained. "Soon as she heard you were okay after the accident, she insisted on cooking y'all a hearty dinner. You know how she is."

And Lilah was no doubt dying to meet his new, live-in partner. He and Harlan exchanged an amused glance. She was curious as a cat, and nothing deterred her from exploring the unknown. A trait that had almost cost Lilah her life.

"Here's something for you to think about, Sheriff," Charlotte suddenly said. "Those men who chased us were tipped off that we were exploring Falling Rock. Soon as we announced at the office that we were going to patrol the area, the men were lying in wait. It's time you considered whether one of your own officers alerted them."

Harlan's spine straightened, and his jaw clenched. Oh, hell, he took those kinds of remarks personally and was about to flip. After the corruption of the previous sheriff, he was hypersensitive to criticism. "Could have been the gatekeeper or just plain bad luck," James said quickly, hoping to diffuse the bomb before it went off.

Charlotte shot him a thanks-for-backing-me-up smirk. "Sticking your head in the sand never helps the situation."

"Don't be so quick to judge," Harlan said, snapping his fingers. "I run a clean operation and personally vetted every officer when I became sheriff."

"Still doesn't mean one of your staff isn't on the take," Charlotte said.

Harlan jerked the car to an abrupt halt.

James opened the back door, eager to forestall the argument. "Thanks for the lift. We'll see you in the morning."

Charlotte shot Harlan another sharp glance but climbed out without further comment.

Before James could follow her, Harlan muttered, "Like to speak to you a moment. In private."

Great. Just what he needed after this long, hellacious day. "Be there in a minute," he called to Charlotte. She continued walking to the porch without bothering to turn around and acknowledge him.

"No wonder she's been suspended for insubordination," Harlan remarked drily.

He leaped to her defense. "Look, she's got trust issues, okay? Probably had a few rats and sour deals go down after all those years working undercover. Their lives depend on suspecting the worst of everyone."

"I don't give a damn about her attitude. It's her…state of mind that concerns me. I spoke with her boss today in Atlanta. He insinuated Detective Helms has emotional issues. Her behavior has been erratic of late—refusing to be reassigned new duties, anger with a couple of other cops she claimed abandoned her during a drug bust, and taking an interest in one particular victim way too personally."

"Her best friend's daughter is one of the kidnapped children. You can't blame her for refusing to give up and taking it to heart. Didn't you take it personally when Lilah was in danger?"

Harlan blew out a deep breath. "Yeah, that's true. You don't have to keep bringing that up."

"And you broke every rule J.D. laid down during his past few weeks as sheriff. You even managed to get yourself fired. Imagine if another agency looked at your record during that time to evaluate your trustworthiness as a potential employee."

"Point taken."

James stuck his hands in his jacket and stared ahead. "There's something you should know. I messed up today. I was in pursuit of those men, but when I got near their vehicle and smelled gasoline...well, I froze."

"The PTSD got to you?"

"Yeah. I warned you about it before I took the job. If you want my badge, it's yours."

Harlan stared straight ahead, as well. "Still seeing that counselor?"

"Twice a month."

He nodded. "If it gets worse, or you want out, let me know. Until then, I have no complaints about your job performance. The men probably would have escaped no matter what."

"We'll never know. But I wanted to set the record straight. I'm the screwup around here, not Charlotte."

Harlan gave him a considering appraisal. "Don't think I haven't noticed the way you've been looking at her. Just remember that she's only here temporarily."

He knew that, but Harlan's warning still twisted his gut.

"She might as well be from across the country," Harlan continued. "The differences between here and Atlanta couldn't be greater."

"I *know*," he said wearily. "I'm not stupid enough to think she'd ever want to stay in Lavender Mountain." Unless one was born and raised in Appalachia, it wasn't an area one often wanted to move *to*—usually, people want to move *out*. He understood this. And Charlotte wasn't seeing the mountains at their greenest and proudest time of year, either.

"This is ridiculous," he muttered, more to himself than Harlan. "I barely know her."

"That's the spirit," Harlan said as James headed to the porch. "Tell my wife not to stay too long, ya hear?"

As if Lilah would listen to either one of them. She pretty much did as she pleased.

He waved a hand in dismissal and entered the house. The scent of chicken and dumplings almost made him weak in the knees. He hadn't even realized he was hungry.

Charlotte was already seated at the kitchen table and blowing on a spoon to cool the dumplings. "I'm starving," she admitted. "Your sister is an angel."

"You might be the first to ever call her that," he said with a snort. "Where's Ellie?" Lilah was almost never without his niece on her hip.

"With the babysitter," said Lilah. "She's under the weather, so I didn't want to take her out."

"What's wrong?" he asked quickly. He hated that little Ellie wasn't her usual bright, babbling self. He'd never figured himself for the liking-kids type, but since the day she was born, Ellie had enchanted him.

"A bit of a cold and sore throat. She'll be fine."

Assured Ellie was going to be okay, he fixed a bowl of dumplings and sat across from Charlotte. Under the kitchen light, her red hair shone with a heat that his fingers itched to stroke. The bright warmth of the kitchen and intimacy of the home-cooked meal loosened the tension of the day.

He could get used to this.

And that scared him more than any high-speed chase.

"WE NEED TO do something about this. James told me your red hair really stood out. It's beautiful, but not practical for undercover work, huh?" Lilah reached across the table and twirled a strand of Charlotte's hair. "Picked up some temporary hair dye for you in town, the brown tank tops you requested and a few little extra somethings."

If by "a few little somethings" she meant underwear, Charlotte would be eternally grateful. She hadn't packed enough clothes, and there'd been no time to do laundry, which landed her in a desperate situation. Going commando wasn't her style.

James stood and peeked in the store bags on the counter, then pulled out a box. "Are you going blond or brunette?"

Charlotte eyed it warily. "Appears I'm going brunette." A wig would have been simpler and less fuss, but this wouldn't be her first dye job to go under the radar.

James continued rustling about in the bag.

"There's nothing in there for you," Lilah said. "Stop—"

He pulled out a six-pack of women's panties and a box of tampons. He dropped both items back into the bag as if it'd scalded his fingers and handed the purchases to Charlotte. "For you," he said drily.

"There's a peach pie for dessert," Lilah commented. "Why don't you get some and go watch television or something?"

"You don't have to tell me twice to get out of the way," he mumbled.

Charlotte suppressed a giggle before a wave of nostalgia washed over her. How long had it been since she'd enjoyed sparring with her two brothers? She did a quick mental calculation. It'd been two Christmases ago.

Way too long.

"Shall we get started?" Lilah asked, opening the hair color box and eyeing the directions.

"No need. I've done this before."

Disappointed blue eyes nailed her. "But I want to help. I've been shut in with a sick baby for two days and could use some serious girl time."

Dang. James's sister was as easy to like as he was. But Harlan's scowling face came to mind. "Your husband probably wants you to head on home."

"Harlan? Nah." She flicked her wrist. "His supper's in the oven, and he can fend for himself for one evening."

Was it wrong that she took a little pleasure in Harlan's forced solitude? She rose and headed to the bathroom. "Let's do this."

Ten minutes later, Charlotte cracked the bathroom window to air out the peroxide fumes. She wrinkled her nose at the mirrored reflection. The dye looked like shellacked tar coating her locks. This couldn't be good. "Maybe we should rinse this out in twenty minutes instead of thirty," she said, dubiously eyeing the mess.

Lilah bit her lip. "The saleslady helped me pick out the color. Made it sound real easy, too."

"It'll be fine," Charlotte reassured her, adjusting the towel around her neck. "It's just hair. It can always be fixed."

"If you say so."

Her tone did not inspire confidence.

Charlotte emptied out the shopping bag, glad to see all the essentials—panties, tampons, shampoo, conditioner, body wash. "Thanks so much."

"You need anything else, let me know. Do you already have a dress for the fund-raiser party?"

"I've got one in my Atlanta apartment I can fetch later. You going?"

"As the sheriff's wife, it's expected. Besides the cash infusion for Harlan's office, those property owners wield lots of political power. Much as my husband hates politics, it'd be foolish not to hobnob with them."

No wonder everyone was so cautious about descending on Falling Rock. "Wouldn't want to tick them off in any way," she slowly agreed.

Lilah nodded. "Not unless absolutely necessary. But Harlan will do whatever it takes to solve this case. Even if it means angering the wrong people."

"He's told you about the trafficking ring?"

"Of course. The whole thought of something

so evil happening close by makes me sick." Lilah shrugged and took a deep breath. "I didn't come to talk shop. Y'all have enough of that on the job. Honestly, I'm looking forward to the fund-raising ball. Wouldn't miss it for the world. I've never gone before. Last year, I had the baby the night before the ball."

"They hire musicians?"

"Only the best. Or so I've heard." Her eyes grew dreamy. "I've always wanted to go inside one of the mansions on Blood Mountain. When I was a little girl, I thought the whole neighborhood was a fairyland of castles."

"Surprised you've never had the opportunity to go in one over the years."

The dreamy expression vanished. "Me? Not hardly."

"Why?"

Lilah let out a long sigh. "You're not from around here, so you wouldn't know. But you've seen the tiny cabin where I grew up. For a whole lot of reasons, the Tedder name isn't one to land you a ticket to a fancy ball."

"Sounds like class bias is everywhere."

"It wasn't just the poverty," Lilah explained. "James hasn't told you our illustrious family history? I thought you two were close."

"He hasn't said much." Charlotte hesitated to bring up the past, but Lilah had broached it first.

"I do read the papers, though. The serial killer incident made the Atlanta news."

Lilah's blue eyes darkened, but in spite of the painful memory, she seemed to quickly shrug it off. "Growing up in our household wasn't easy. My dad was a moonshiner with a monster temper, and my parents argued constantly until Mom moved out."

"I'm sorry. James hasn't mentioned any of that to me. Look, I don't want you to get the wrong idea about us. We're business partners. And I'm grateful to him for helping me with this case, of course."

Lilah raised a brow. "That's all there is to it?"

She flushed, thinking of his kisses. "What has he told you about me?"

"Nothing. But anyone can see the sparks between you two. And it's more than that. I've seen the way he looks at you."

She couldn't stop the warm glow that lit her belly or the smile that lifted her lips. "Really?"

"Positive. I've worried about James since he returned from Afghanistan. He's been withdrawn and alone for too long."

The warm glow faded. "You know I work undercover. Our living together is temporary. I won't be staying long."

"Atlanta's not so far you can't visit on weekends," Lilah said. "You have to come back to

Lavender Mountain in the spring, when the whole forest comes alive. Or the fall, when the leaves are changing color. Right now, we're not at our best."

Lilah sounded as if she worked at the local tourist office. "I'm sure it's beautiful. But working undercover isn't like being a regular cop. I can't always come and go as I please. It's not a job. It's a lifestyle."

"Sounds extremely demanding and not much fun."

Fun? No. The fun had worn off years ago. Charlotte couldn't remember the last time she found it even remotely pleasurable. But she did important work. Work that few others wanted to take on.

Ding. The portable kitchen timer startled them both.

That time had gone by quickly. After rinsing the dye, Charlotte realized she'd have to eat her earlier words about it being "just hair" that could always "be fixed."

Lilah let out a startled wail.

Charlotte's formerly auburn locks were now a mess of tangled black straw. All she needed was a hawk of a nose and a wart on her chin for a perfect Halloween witch disguise.

Too bad it was November.

A knock rapped the bathroom door. "Everything okay in there?" James asked.

Quickly she wrapped her ruined hair up in a turban. The guy was probably impatient for a shower. "One minute," she called out.

"Sorry," Lilah breathed.

"No big deal. During work hours, I always wear it in a ponytail anyway."

Lilah washed and dried her hands and opened the door. "Guess I'll be heading home now. Ellie might wake up feeling miserable and want me." Her face lit up. "Have I showed you her picture?" Without waiting for an answer, Lilah lifted her purse from the table and pulled out a cell phone.

James groaned. "Here we go."

"Just one quick look," his sister promised, holding out the phone to Charlotte.

Ellie's toothless grin and folds of baby fat were typical, but the crystal blue eyes were not. They were the startling blue shared by James and Lilah. She'd recognize that shade anywhere.

The towel slipped from her hair and dropped to the floor.

James stared at her, eyes wide and jaw slack. "What happened to your hair?" he asked, voice booming.

Lilah poked her brother in the side and scowled.

"I mean... I'm sure it'll look better when it dries," he amended.

"Sure." Like hell it would. She sat down at the table and felt the tangled tumbleweed of hair. The damage might be beyond repair. Maybe she should cut it supershort. Absently she said good-bye to Lilah, and the door opened and closed.

James sat down beside her. "So...you got some conditioner? Darla—my other sister—once had a dye job disaster. She went around the house slathered in hair conditioner for a week to repair the damage."

Charlotte sucked in her breath at the mention of Darla. That sister's name had been all over the news last year. She couldn't imagine how much it would hurt if something tragic happened with her brothers—no matter how big of a pain in the ass they could be. "Yeah, Lilah bought a bottle. It's in the bathroom."

He rose from the table and returned with it in hand. "Let's see what we can do."

Before she could protest, he poured half the bottle in her hair and gently ran his fingers over the knots.

"You don't have to—"

"Shhh...relax," he whispered.

His fingers pressed into her scalp and neck, massaging and caressing. She closed her eyes and gave herself up to the pleasure of the moment. Not even cold glops of conditioner running down her face and nape deterred from the comfort of his touch.

A vision of Ellie's blue eyes flashed through her mind, and a primitive urge to procreate clenched her gut. Hell, she hadn't known she had a biological clock. That wasn't anywhere on her radar.

Until now.

That realization almost made her want to run from the hills.

Chapter Eight

"The bloodwork came in," James announced at his office the next morning, slamming the phone down. "That was no deer killed in the woods. The blood was human."

Charlotte's face paled, and panic lit her eyes. "It wasn't... It can't be Jenny's. Maybe someone's just been injured—"

He hastened to reassure her. "We won't have the DNA results for weeks. And it's not necessarily from any of the captive girls. Anyone could have had an accident on a four-wheeler."

"We checked the hospitals and clinics. No serious accidents were reported near the vicinity. It *has* to be one of those girls."

Privately he agreed, but kept his mouth shut. "We'll find out soon enough. Harlan wants us and Sammy in his office right now to work out a plan."

As they scurried down the hall, their coworker

joined them midway. "What the hell?" Sammy asked, pointing to Charlotte's hair.

"Red hair is a little too conspicuous," she answered stiffly. "I took corrective measures."

James stifled a grin at her tight French braid. But Charlotte could dye her hair green and purple, and it wouldn't detract from her beauty one iota.

Zelda was seated by Harlan's desk, taking notes. "Subpoena the gatekeeper's records," Harlan ordered.

She adjusted the glasses on the bridge of her nose. "How far back ya want me to go?"

"At least a year."

Zelda nodded and left the room.

"Let's hit the ground running today," Harlan announced, slapping his hands on the desk. "I won't have my officers blindsided again like y'all were yesterday." He slid a pair of car keys across the table. "Here's your new vehicle. A temporary loaner from Floyd County until the destroyed cruiser is replaced. James and Detective Helms will canvass the Falling Rock neighborhood today, show photos of the Ashbury girl, and see if anyone's spotted her, or if their reaction is suspicious. Sammy, I want you to—"

Charlotte abruptly stood. "No. This isn't a good idea."

James shook his head. She never ceased to

surprise him. "I thought you'd want to take action. You've been champing at the bit ever since you got here."

"If we do this, the traffickers will know something's up, and they'll find a way to transport the girls out."

"We can have an officer watch the gate to search any suspicious vehicles that leave," he suggested.

"What about the dirt path out back? If we give them any wiggle room, we can kiss the whole operation goodbye. I've been tracking them for over a damn year, and I won't have the girls' lives jeopardized."

He stood as well, standing toe to toe with her. So much for last night's détente. "Nobody wants that. But we can't just sit on our asses and do nothing."

Charlotte turned to Harlan. "Can't you do something to speed up those DNA results? All we need is one concrete piece of evidence for a judge."

"So, what's your great plan?" James interrupted, stung at her quick dismissal of him. "Keep sitting out in the woods every day and hoping Jenny or one of the others happens to look out the window again?"

Her face flushed, staining her cheeks crimson.

"Simmer down, you two," Harlan said.

They breathed hard, staring at one another. Sammy gave a low, amused whistle.

"I said sit *down*," Harlan thundered. "Last I checked, I'm the one running this show, and I'll decide what strategy to take."

James felt like a chastened schoolboy as he settled back in his chair.

"Now, here's what we're going to do. Sammy will guard the back of the Stowerses' property to make sure no one leaves via four-wheelers or a jeep on those back roads. He'll let us know at once if there's any suspicious activity."

"There are lives at stake here," Charlotte cautioned. "I know we all want to rush in and rescue them." Her fists clenched and unclenched by her sides. "But they're in a volatile situation. We can't make it worse for them by arousing premature suspicion. I say we keep an eye out from afar until the fund-raiser. Monitor the gate to make sure no one enters or exits Falling Rock to ensure that the captives stay where they are. Then, at the fund-raiser, we all spread out and find what we can inside the Stowerses' house."

"Search without a warrant? Highly illegal," James pointed out. "And how are we supposed to get in there?"

"You said they always had lots of out-of-town guests staying over for the event. There's bound to be lots of foot traffic between their place and the clubhouse. We'll try and blend in with the crowd."

"And we don't have to exactly call it a search," Harlan said slowly. "I'd phrase it more like *keeping our eyes open*. If you know what I mean."

"You can call it what you want. I won't leave until I've gone through every room in that house," Charlotte retorted.

"Ditto," James agreed. "Although I still don't see the harm in questioning the neighborhood today about who might have been driving that black sedan and if anyone's seen Jenny Ashbury. Only good can come when a community is alerted. Plus, it'll make future trafficking that much harder to slip by unnoticed if residents are on the lookout for unusual activity." James turned to Sammy. "What do you think?"

"I say let's head out there now." Sammy gave Charlotte an apologetic smile. "Sorry, Detective. Looks like you're in the minority."

She ran a hand over the black wisps of hair that had escaped her braid. "At least let me be the one to question the Stowerses. That is, if they even answer the door."

"Not alone, you aren't," James said quickly. Did she think she could brush aside their partnership so easily? Hurt, mixed equally with anger, coursed through his body.

"I can handle it," she said curtly. "I've been

doing this kind of work for years. Much longer than you have."

Ouch. Bitten in the ass by his own logic.

"You'll go together," Harlan ordered. "It shouldn't be me. The Stowerses would view a personal visit by the sheriff as more threatening and suspicious. They might be more open with James."

"Doubt that," James muttered. "If you're hoping they'll invite me in for coffee and cookies, then you've forgotten what the Tedder name means around here."

Harlan shrugged. "Times are changing." His eyes and face softened. "A lot of that is thanks to Lilah. She has a real way with people."

Sammy stood. "Shall we get started?"

They all rose, and Harlan passed out copies of Jenny's photo. "Zelda got copies ready for us this morning. I'll form a blockade by the gatehouse and personally check every vehicle that passes by. Everyone all set?"

They nodded and left his office. It was a tense walk to their new department-issued vehicle. James opened the door and Charlotte edged up to him.

"Why don't I drive today?"

"I'm more familiar with the area. An advantage if another vehicle tails us again."

She didn't look happy about his answer, but walked over to the passenger side and got in. He faced Charlotte before starting the car. "Why all the hostility in there? Thought we were a team."

"That doesn't mean I quietly accept ideas that I think are wrong."

"I can't believe you're opposed to this questioning. You've been raring for action."

"I've already expressed my reservations. No need to rehash the issue. Let me do the talking when we get to the Stowerses'."

"No way," he said, starting the engine and backing out of the parking space. "The cover story is that you're a new trainee. It'll look suspicious if you take the lead."

"Oh, alright," she conceded in a huff. "I can admit when I'm wrong. You take the lead."

"Thank you."

They didn't speak again until the Falling Rock gatehouse came into view. Charlotte placed a hand on his arm. "Sorry you felt attacked in there," she said quietly. "I just… I can't screw this up."

He took her hand and gave it a quick squeeze. "I know what this case means to you and to Jenny's mother. I'd never do anything to jeopardize the girl's safety."

Charlotte nodded. "And James, there's no one I'd rather do this with than you."

SHE MIGHT HAVE been opposed to the plan, but Charlotte's heart skipped with excitement as they walked up the stone pathway to the Stowerses' house. Most of the neighbors hadn't been home today, but the few that were claimed no knowledge of a black sedan and said they didn't recognize Jenny's photo. But that was what they'd expected, anyway.

This was it. The real reason for questioning Falling Rock residents. She was walking on the very ground where Jenny was being held against her will.

James quirked a brow. "I'm lead. Right?"

"Right," she said grudgingly, stuffing her hands in the brown uniform jacket. Besides the fact that it would look suspicious for a trainee to do most of the talking, her personal involvement might make her too aggressive in questioning and blow up the case.

The front door was a massive wooden showpiece, hand-carved with a mountain range design. James rang the doorbell, which seemed to echo in the cavernous interior.

A petite older lady answered the door, wearing a gray dress with a spotless white apron. Her once-auburn hair was streaked with gray and pulled back into a tight bun. She even wore a frilly lace maid's cap like Charlotte had seen only in the movies.

Fear snapped in the woman's dark eyes. "May I help you?" she asked with a strong accent that Charlotte couldn't quite place. Irish, perhaps, given the red hair and fair skin.

"May we speak to the lady of the house?" James asked.

"One moment. I'll go see."

The ornate door closed, and Charlotte shared a look with James. The sound of it clicking shut echoed in the pit of her stomach like doom. She might have been opposed to the visit originally, but getting this close—only to be denied entrance—was excruciating.

Yet she said nothing and stared straight ahead. You never knew when cameras or audio tapes might be rolling. If she were in the traffickers' position, she'd certainly take those precautions.

A staccato percussion sounded on the hard floor, and the door creaked open. "Hello, officers," said Madeline Stowers. "To what do I owe the pleasure?"

Long silver hair was loosely gathered at her nape in a stylish coif that was much too elegant to have been accidental. Self-consciously, Charlotte touched her hand to her own dyed hack job.

Maddie's face was beautiful and possessed the underlying bone structure of a model's, although a faint tightness suggested plastic surgery accounted in part for the firm, barely wrinkled skin. Her brown eyes were wide and her eyebrows thin and arched. A tasteful shade of rose-red glistened on her lips. She wore a black shirt with a deep V that belted at the waist and a black pencil skirt that highlighted her slim physique.

"Mrs. Stowers?" James asked.

"Call me Maddie." She glanced at their nametags. "Officers Tedder and Hanson?" Her slight frown did nothing to mar the smooth plane of her forehead.

Botox, Charlotte guessed.

"Yes, ma'am," James answered. "May we come in?"

It took willpower not to sneak a surprised glance his way. A bold move. He hadn't requested to enter anyone else's home.

A heartbeat of hesitation, and then, "Of course, do come in." Maddie stepped aside and waved them along with a graceful sweep of an arm.

Charlotte entered and picked up a familiar, powdery-sweet scent of black violets mixed with citrus. Maddie used the same brand of designer perfume that her late grandmother once favored. They passed through the foyer and entered the den. She felt her jaw drop, but she couldn't contain her split-second reaction to the opulence. This was a whole new criminal class from what she was normally accustomed to dealing with.

Usually the ones she sought undercover lived in squalor in a crack house or some back alley.

The entire back wall was covered in plate-glass windows that afforded a stunning view of trees and mountains. Everywhere she looked, from the paneled, beamed ceilings and walls to the fireplace, the house consisted of custom wood, glass or stone. The only exception was the rustic touch of a twisting iron staircase that led upstairs.

The mountain outdoor element also continued indoors, so much so that even a water element was featured by a huge, man-made rock water-fall that poured into a custom inlaid pool edged with stone and set by the crackling fireplace. The faint scent of burning oak gave the place a ski resort vibe. Two rolled towels were set by the pool, an invitation to indulge in luxury.

"Please, come have a seat," Maddie said, leading them to a leather sectional sofa that could easily accommodate a dozen people. "I take it you're here to discuss some aspect of the fund-raiser? I'm surprised the sheriff didn't contact me directly, though."

"No, ma'am. That's not why we're here," James said.

Charlotte sank onto the sofa next to him while Maddie seated herself opposite, crossing her long legs and smoothing the front of her skirt.

"Sounds ominous," she said with a tinkling laugh. "It's usually so peaceful here. That's why Richard and I bought this place, to escape the noise and the crowds of Atlanta. Don't even get me started on the city traffic. The older we get, the more time we seem to spend here at Falling Rock. Excuse my manners. Would you care for some coffee?"

"Yes—" Charlotte began.

"No." James shrugged. "Okay, coffee would be great. Thanks."

Maddie turned her head and motioned to the maid. "Colleen, serve us coffee and a few slices of that lemon pound cake the chef baked this morning." She faced them again. "It's loaded with sugar, but delicious. Do try a piece."

Hard to believe the perfect woman in front of them ever ate anything but carrots and tofu. She must have an iron will to keep that figure with a pastry chef in the house, Charlotte mused.

James pulled a five-by-seven photograph of Jenny from his coat pocket. "Do you know this person?"

Maddie took the photo and examined it for several seconds. "No. Sorry. Is she in some sort of trouble?"

"She's been missing for two weeks," James said.

Damn, Charlotte had to give it to him. He

might have been working in law enforcement for only a few months, but he had the poker face of an officer experienced at interrogating people.

"That poor girl," Maddie cooed, returning the photo. "I take it she's from Lavender Mountain?"

"No, metro Atlanta," Charlotte piped in.

"Is that so?" One perfectly tweezed brow arched, again with no accompanying wrinkles.

It was freaky, Charlotte decided. Unnatural.

"Why on earth are you looking for her way out here, then?" Maddie asked, directing her attention at James. "Does she have family in the area?"

"We're following a tip," he commented, giving nothing away.

"Hard to believe she's landed in such a remote area. I'd imagine strangers in our community would be easily noticeable, at least during this time of year, with the tourist season over."

"So you'd think," James agreed. "But so far, no one's claimed to have seen her."

"Then I'm afraid your tip must have been a bad one. Perhaps an attempt to steer you in the wrong direction?"

James nodded. "That's very astute of you."

Oh, yes, the man was definitely good at his job. Charlotte stood and casually stretched her shoulders. "That's an amazing view you have here," she said, stepping over to the windows against the back wall. Down below, she observed four muscled men dressed in jeans and sporting navy T-shirts. They'd obviously stepped up their security game. She squinted but failed to spot Sammy. Wherever he was staked out, he'd done a fine job of camouflaging his presence.

"It is lovely, isn't it? Ah, Colleen, that was quick. Thank you."

The maid set down a tray on the coffee table and then quickly left the room as Maddie leaned over to pour.

"I'd like to wash up first," Charlotte said. "If you don't mind."

"Down the hall and fifth door on your left," Maddie replied with apparent unconcern.

A quick glance at James's face showed a caution warning in his eyes. He might be a good officer, but this wasn't her first search. Well, technically, this was *not* a search. It was a mere observation of the property that could be legally obtained through a casual stroll.

She slowly walked down the hallway, grateful for the open doors. She passed three bedrooms, each huge with large windows and carpet that appeared to be inches thick, the kind that would feel like walking on pillows. The furniture was heavy wood, and the dressers were empty of any sign that someone actually slept there.

She looked up in the corners of the hallways

and bedrooms, curious to see if there were any cameras. Nothing obvious, though they could be cleverly hidden and out of sight. But if she were caught spying on their camera, she could claim she'd mistakenly taken a wrong turn.

Charlotte stepped into one of the bedrooms. The carpeting was as plush as she'd imagined. She halted in the middle of the room, furrowing her brow as if she'd mistakenly entered. If nothing else, a decent undercover cop knew how to put on an act.

But her side excursion didn't help. The closet doors were shut, and even on the opposite side of the dresser bureau, there was no stray clothing or any strewn item to suggest a person used the room. No, the girls were more likely locked in a basement as Karen had claimed—although these bedrooms on the main floor might be used by potential clients to "try out the wares."

The mere thought stiffened her spine and strengthened her resolve to save Jenny. Charlotte left the room and located the bathroom. Gleaming white bounced from walls to ceiling with marble tiles, counters and flooring. As much as she admired the cozy opulence of the rest of the main floor, the white-on-white décor smacked too much of a sterile hospital to suit her tastes.

A camera in here would be inappropriate in all kind of ways, but anyone who kidnapped teenage girls for trafficking was not above installing a discreet bathroom camera. Charlotte leisurely washed her hands and let her eyes rove. Again, everything was meticulously clean and devoid of human personality. She opened cabinet drawers stocked with unopened toothbrushes and toothpaste for guests. The far-left drawer held a pewter hairbrush, but the few hairs in it were long and silver—Maddie's. Charlotte strained her ears, opening her senses to even the faintest whisper.

But only James's and Maddie's voices droned from the den. Disappointed, she returned to them. James fired a quick inquiring glance over his coffee cup, and she shook her head in an almost imperceptible move.

"Will you be in attendance at the fund-raiser?" Maddie asked. "We always invite the officers and their families, even young children. That is, if they're old enough to be awake in the later hours of the evening. It's a real family affair."

"Wouldn't miss it," he declared.

"Me neither," Charlotte said, sitting down by James. "Rookies are invited, too, I take it."

Maddie's smile never wavered, but a cold snap flashed for a second in her dark eyes. "Of course, dear."

So the platinum witch was one of those who viewed other females as competition. That, or

Maddie had somehow guessed her true identity. Game on. Charlotte picked up her coffee cup and settled into the cushions, as if intending to make herself at home for a very long time.

"I hear there will be live music." Charlotte sipped the black coffee. "I can't speak for any of the other officers, but I plan on dancing until the music stops and the maids have to shoo me away at dawn."

"Lovely," Maddie said drily, shifting her attention back to James. "I heard about the commotion yesterday near Falling Rock. So shocking. Hope the officers involved are all okay?"

"We're both fine."

"Oh? It was you and—" Maddie leaned forward and scrutinized Charlotte's badge. "Officer Bailey Hanson."

Her name on the badge was a fake. A precautionary measure.

Charlotte lifted her chin. "We're still kicking. Obviously. Not so sure about the other guys, though. Any of your men show up hurt today, by chance?"

Maddie blinked. "As far as I know, they're just fine. You suspect one of them was involved in the incident?"

She made a mental note to ask Sammy if any of the workers outside looked as if they'd suffered injuries.

"It could be anyone," James said. "We've been talking to everyone in the neighborhood who's home."

Charlotte helped herself to a slice of the pound cake and bit into the buttery goodness. "Yum. This is delicious. Will you be catering the fund-raiser?"

"Of course. The menu's set. We'll have hors d'oeuvres and shrimp canapés and tea cakes. Plenty of champagne, as well."

Charlotte turned to James. "That should keep us all busy."

"What do you mean?" Maddie asked.

"All the catering and staff coming in and out of here will be monitored. We've set up camp at the gatehouse to record every vehicle and person that enters and exits Falling Rock. Can't be too careful. Kidnappers are on the loose." Charlotte set her plate down with a clatter. Let Maddie stew over that bit of information.

James stood. "See you soon, Mrs. Stowers. Thanks for the coffee."

Maddie stood, as well, smoothing down the front of her skirt again, then following them to the door. "My pleasure. We'll look forward to the event. Richard and I always enjoy this occasion. It's the least we can do to give back to this community. Lavender Mountain is our little home away from home. I understand that the proceeds from our event provides as much as twenty-five percent of your annual budget."

Charlotte almost snorted. Way to plug her political influence.

"The sheriff, and all of us, are most grateful," James said.

"I believe in giving back."

Charlotte hated the self-righteous tone of Maddie's voice.

"In Atlanta, I do lots of volunteer work, as well," the woman continued. "My favorite is working at the teen suicide hotline. So many young lives in crisis."

Charlotte's nerve endings tingled, and her mouth went dry.

James nodded. "Thank you for your service."

Maddie closed the door softly behind them, and Charlotte followed James to the cruiser. Inside, he turned to her. "What gives? I saw you tense up there at the end."

"The crisis hotline. My source about the Stowerses? Karen Hicks was suicidal and had called a hotline for help not long before she was kidnapped."

"Well," he said, starting the car, "it appears we've found our Pied Piper."

Chapter Nine

"Why are we stopping here?" Charlotte asked.

James mentally shook himself and stared at his father's cabin. Yet again, it seemed like the old homestead drew him even when he had no conscious plan to visit. Not that he'd admit that to Charlotte. It smacked of a weak character.

"Thought we'd visit Sammy. Check to see if any of the Stowerses' men have shown signs of injury. See if there's anything unusual."

She shrugged. "Beats doing nothing."

Her voice sounded as discouraged as his thoughts. For the last several days, all their knocking on doors and combing through the gatekeeper's records had yielded nothing other than an immediate complaint from the Falling Rock management corporation and the ire of the residents.

"My four-wheeler's still parked in the shed. Shouldn't take too long to go have a look."

Dispiritedly, Charlotte tagged along beside

him as he pulled out the ATV. The case weighed heavily on her. For several nights, he couldn't help overhearing bits and pieces of Charlotte's conversation with her friend, Tanya. She'd tried to convey optimism, but after hanging up the phone, her face would be tight and withdrawn.

He knew that helpless feeling. When his own family had been in crisis, he'd been stuck in Afghanistan and unable to protect his sisters. Sometimes at night, he had lain awake on his cot, and worry had buzzed his brain like a storm of hungry gnats.

If she was anything like him—and he suspected Charlotte was—then the best cure was to keep busy, keep digging and poking even when there seemed no point. Even the tiniest clue could often make or break a case.

Charlotte zipped her uniform jacket all the way up and donned gloves and earmuffs. "You're not worried about blowing Sammy's cover?"

"Not particularly." He started the engine, and it sparked to life on the second try. "They already know we're watching them," he explained, raising his voice above the running motor. "Hop on."

She climbed on the back seat, and the contact of her body against his made him grit his teeth. Never had he once imagined being turned on by a partner when he entered into the life of an easygoing, small-town deputy. His dream of a quiet life wasn't panning out, but as he ran over a rut and Charlotte's body bounced against his back, James knew he wouldn't want it any other way.

He accelerated the engine. Trees and shrubs raced past his vision, and the chill mountain air invigorated his body and spirits. The land here never failed him—it was vast and constant, and every hill and hollow was imprinted in his DNA. His old army buddies questioned his decision to return to Lavender Mountain, but James knew this was his home, his land. The place he belonged.

He almost drove right past Sammy, who'd parked his camouflaged ATV behind a dense clump of evergreens. Only the sun glinting off the binocular lenses gave away his location. No surprise there. Sammy and Harlan and he used to hunt together, and each knew how to blend into the woods. James drew up beside him.

"Trying to blow my cover?" Sammy asked, but his eyes held their usual good humor.

"Doesn't much matter. They know we're keeping watch."

"Anything new happening?"

"Not a damn thing," Charlotte said, swinging one leg over the side and stepping down to the ground. "I want to nail Maddie Stowers so bad. She has the moral compass of a sociopath."

"The steel magnolia type, eh?" Sammy asked.

"In an evil way, yes. My theory is that Maddie often finds vulnerable, at-risk girls while working at a teen suicide hotline and then lures them into the trafficking ring. Either that or she preys on the homeless…whoever she can find who's vulnerable. Seen any unusual activity?"

"Nope. Just these men half-assed picking up broken branches and debris. Must be paid by the hour," he joked.

"Nobody staring out the window?"

James's heart pinched. She was desperate to know Jenny was alive and well.

"Sorry, Detective. Nothing."

James took the binoculars from Sammy's hands and stared at the crew. None appeared scratched-up or marred as though they'd experienced a near-fatal car crash days ago. But the Stowerses certainly had enough resources to keep hiring as many men as needed to maintain security. If one or two went down, they could easily hire more staff as replacements. Human trafficking was a lucrative business.

He recalled the immense house with its indoor heated pool and every other amenity for two people who lived there only part-time. No doubt their Atlanta mansion was just as opulent. And all of it earned off the misery of abused children.

Charlotte tugged at his jacket sleeve. "What do you see? My turn."

He handed her the binoculars and climbed back on the ATV. "Guess we'll go for a spin down the road a bit," he told Sammy. "Check out the area."

Charlotte sighed and returned the field glasses.

Again he reveled in the weight of her body braced against his as they rode, the ATV shaking and pitching in the deeply rutted dirt path. But as they rounded the curve leading away from Falling Rock, Charlotte yelled, "Stop!" waving an arm and pointing behind her.

James slammed on the brakes, and the ATV spun in a semicircle, sending up bits of mud and leaves. "What is it?"

"Over there, near the edge of the clearing. There are two men with shovels and a garbage bag. Do you think—"

"That they're digging a shallow grave?" He thought of the spilled blood they'd found earlier in the week. "Yeah. Could be. Or could they might be 'sengers."

"What's that?"

"I'll explain later." James stepped on the gas and reversed direction. "Let's find out which it is."

The two men abruptly stopped digging and eyed them warily. The eldest, sporting a long gray beard, hugged a garbage bag to his chest as he high-tailed it to a four-wheeler. The other guy, who looked young enough to be his son, or even grandson, dropped both his shovel and bag and also made a beeline for their mud-splattered vehicle.

"Halt!" James yelled.

Their old motor engine turned over once, then twice, before it started. James pulled in beside them, and the old man reached for a shotgun mounted on the hood.

Damn it. The old coot had a couple of seconds' bead on him. No way he could stop his ATV and withdraw his sidearm before he was already looking down the barrel of the mountain man's shotgun.

"Drop it!" Charlotte commanded. She half fell off the back seat, and then landed on her feet like a cat, gun drawn and aimed.

A blur of brown came between him and the old dude.

"Hell, no." The old man abandoned the attempt to grab his weapon and hit the gas. The old contraption lurched forward.

This was a chase the men had no chance of winning. "Get back on," he ordered Charlotte.

"Hell with that." She fired a warning shot, the blast echoing through the hollow.

The younger man glanced back, eyes round as a full moon. The ATV jerked to the right. The driver had enough smarts to get off the main path and try to lose them in the woods.

Charlotte dropped her weapon. "I had a shot at their back tire, but he switched directions on me at the last minute."

James revved the engine. "Get on. We'll catch them."

Quickly she climbed on board, and he gave chase. Had it been summer, the men might have been able to conceal their whereabouts, using green foliage as camouflage. But in the November barrenness, they were dead meat.

A shot rang out.

Son of a bitch. Did they really expect to get away with shooting two officers of the law in broad daylight? And then escaping on an old ATV that probably had a maximum speed of only thirty miles per hour? What the hell did they think they were doing? If they were guilty of illegally harvesting wild ginseng, as he now suspected, the pickers had way overreacted.

The trail narrowed. Did the men have a plan, or had they fled on a knee-jerk impulse? Soon there would be nowhere left to drive. Worst-case scenario, they were part of a larger group that was nearby and could be recruited to assist their fight. Or maybe there was a drying shed nearby that the men hoped to hole up in.

Both possibilities became moot as the men's four-wheeler crashed into a huge oak.

James drew out his sidearm as he raced forward. This time he'd be ready.

CHARLOTTE'S HEART NEARLY burst with anticipation. They'd get these men and force them to talk. With any luck, they'd provide a clue to help catch the traffickers.

Both men jumped off the ATV, the eldest clutching his shotgun. She and James did likewise with their pistols. But the yahoo mountain outlaws still weren't done fleeing, and the two ran in opposite directions.

So it was going to be one of *those* arrests. Lots of trouble and a real pain in the ass.

"You go after the younger," James shouted.

Of *course* he chose the armed man to chase, and it ticked her off. She was as capable as any male cop when it came to apprehending felons. No time to argue, though. Later she'd set him straight on that score.

Charlotte took off, legs pumping and heart pounding double-time with adrenaline. Fortunately, the past several days had been event-free, allowing her injuries to heal. Problem was, her target was just as hyped as she was.

From below, brambles sliced and shredded her pants legs while low-lying tree branches from above slapped her torso. On and on he ran. Whatever the guy had done, she'd make sure a fleeing arrest charge stick. That and whatever else she could slap on him.

The dude was fast and crafty, darting from tree to tree in a zigzag pattern. She briefly wondered if James had caught up with the old man.

"Stop!" she ordered.

He didn't look back or slow down. The jerk. He wasn't getting away. Not even if it meant her heart exploded from exertion. "You're just making—" Charlotte gulped oxygen into her burning lungs "—it harder on yourself." She drew a few more gasping breaths. "Give it up."

"Up yours," he shouted, flipping her the middle finger.

Nice guy. But she'd seen and heard worse. *Far* worse.

Abruptly the trail widened, and he stumbled into the open. He glanced back at her, eyes bewildered and panicked. Charlotte smiled and raised her gun. "Halt!" she called out. "Got a clear shot" —she panted, though her aim never wavered— "at you this time."

He hesitated, running a hand through his dark, shoulder-length hair, and then raised both arms high in defeat.

Charlotte approached, cautious. She didn't trust his sudden surrender for a second. Backup would be cool right about now, but she was used to working alone. She only hoped Sammy had heard the fired shots and had left his post to find James.

"On the ground," she ordered. "Facedown."

He dropped, and she was pleased to note the rise and fall of his chest. Apparently, the run had tired him out, as well—but he might yet have some fight left in him.

"Hands behind your back, and spread your legs wide."

He grudgingly complied. "Bitch," he muttered, then spit.

"Careful. You might hurt my tender feelings." She stood over him and used her right leg to spread his legs out further. "Got any weapons?"

"If I did, I'd have used 'em on you by now."

Dude was charming. Defiant to the end. She tucked her gun into her side holster and withdrew a pair of handcuffs.

"That ain't necessary."

She bent to one knee and slapped a cuff on his left wrist. "I'll decide what's necessary."

Charlotte grabbed his right wrist, but he twisted and jerked away. He reached into his jacket pocket. Must have a weapon after all. She'd expected no less.

Quickly she rose as he pulled out a knife and flicked it open. Sunlight touched the silver blade, and it glinted with malicious promise. She had one second to prevent an attack that could leave her gutted. Another second, and she'd have to run and would turn from hunter to prey. *Not happening.* Charlotte lifted her right foot and then stomped with all her might on his right hand.

"Owww...son of a bitch!" His fingers loosened their hold on the knife, and he curled into a fetal position. "I think you broke it!"

She stuffed the knife in her pocket, then bent down again and cuffed his wrists together. "What you got here?" Inside his other jacket pocket was yet another knife. "Any more weapons? Tell me now, and I won't have to hurt you again."

"One more knife. Right pants pocket."

She retrieved the weapon and patted down his legs before ordering him to roll over. Swiftly her hands ran down his arms, chest and hips.

"You need to git me to a doc," he said with a pitiful moan.

The adrenaline left her system with a rush, and she sank onto her haunches several yards from his curled-up body. She reached for her walkie-talkie and then let out a moan of her own. Either she'd left it in the truck or had lost it during the chase. Just terrific. "Looks like we're in for a hike."

"Can't," he protested.

"You've got a broken wrist, not a broken leg."

His face flushed scarlet, and his eyes were bright with tears. Whether from pain or anger, she didn't know and didn't much care.

"Heartless bitch. I'm suing your ass. Police brutality."

"That's me. Coldhearted," she cheerily agreed. "Some perp twice my size tries to gut me with a knife, and I dare defend myself. Wonder who the judge and jury will rule for at trial?"

He scrambled to a sitting position, turned his head to the side, and spat again. "There's more than one way to get justice 'round here."

Anger blazed behind her temples, and she stuffed her fists into her jacket. What she really wanted to do was pummel some sense into the guy, but that was a line she'd never cross. In and out she breathed, willing her temper to cool. Dude hit a nerve for sure. This wasn't the first time she'd heard such a threat, and she didn't take it idly. One day her past might catch up to her. She'd return to her one-bedroom apartment some night, and someone would be there, waiting for her in the darkness.

"You want to sit around all day and exchange pleasantries, or shall we return to our ATV? I'm sure Officer Tedder has your partner in custody by now."

"Betcha Grandpa got away." A smirk twisted his thin lips.

Charlotte jumped to her feet. Why was she lollygagging? James might need her assistance. "Rest is over. Time to hit the trail."

"You go. I'll wait here."

"The hell you will." Charlotte leaned over and yanked at his cuffs.

A high-pitched wail escaped his mouth.

"C'mon, big guy," she said as he struggled to his feet. "Play nice, and I won't tell your grandpa and your future cellmates that I made you cry like a girl."

He opened his mouth, no doubt to call her another choice name, but then clamped it shut. "I'm coming," he said, his face scrunched in sullenness.

Frankly, he could pout all he wanted as long as he followed orders. Charlotte made a sweeping gesture. "You go first."

She followed a couple of feet behind as they made their way back through the underbrush. Only the crunch of their shoes and an occasional bird call ruffled the wooded silence. Where was James? With every step, her worry increased.

The crashed ATV came into view, still overturned and lying on its side. And still no sign of James. The cuffed suspect turned and grinned. "What'd I tell ya? Grandpa's long gone."

"Yeah, gone to jail," she snapped. But her uneasiness grew, pinching at her lungs and heart.

One of the large black garbage bags the men carried had fallen two feet from the ATV. What was in them—drugs? Weapons? Body parts? Curious, she scooped it up and looked inside. The bag held...vegetables? She pulled out one of the plants and held it in her palms. It had a green stem about twelve inches long that was topped with five leaves. Long, stringy roots resembling white carrots were attached to the base of the stem.

"What's this? Albino carrots?" she asked.

He snorted. "It's 'seng."

She blinked. "Come again?"

"Ginseng. You ain't never heard of it?"

"It's an herb, right? But...what's the big deal? Why the hell did y'all run from us?"

A voice called from behind, "Because it's highly profitable and highly illegal."

Charlotte whipped her head around. James strode her way, grandpa cuffed beside him. Relief jellied her knees, and for one horrible moment, she thought she might faint. So this must be what Southern belles called a swoon back in the old days. She straightened her shoulders and frowned. Since when had James's well-being mattered as much or more than her own?

She had a job to do here, one that required all her focus.

"Thought you'd got away," the younger guy muttered, clearly disappointed. "Did he rough you up any? I think this one broke my damn wrist."

James quirked a brow at her, amusement dancing in his eyes.

"He neglected to mention he sustained the injury while attempting to stab me," she said.

Her partner's amusement flashed to fury. His eyes were flaming blue orbs, and his whole body grew taut, filling the air with a crackling tension. He left grandpa behind, all his focus on the younger man.

Now the dude wasn't so cocky. He stepped backward and held up his cuffed hands. "I'm hurt," he whined.

James grabbed him up by the collar and pushed his body against a pine.

This was a side of James she'd never seen. "Wait." She tried to wedge herself between the two men. "Stop. I handled the situation. It's over."

James let go but kept glaring at the guy.

A little redirection was in order. She retrieved a pen and small notepad from her uniform shirt. "Okay. Junior claims to need a doctor, so let's get the ball rolling. Y'all have any identification on you?"

Grandpa shook his head. "Don't need it to drive my four-wheeler."

"Name, please." Her pen hovered over the notepad.

"Linton Harold Drexler the Fourth. And this here's my grandson." A grand name for grandpa.

"And yours?" she asked Junior.

"Ross Drexler, you—"

"Careful," James warned with a growl.

She scribbled down the information, then held up the plastic bag. "Ross told me they were digging up ginseng, and that appears to be what's in the bags they carried."

"Yep. If they hadn't resisted arrest, they'd be charged with poaching and trespassing, which usually only carries a small fine."

"You questioned them yet about seeing or hearing anything?"

"We ain't no snitches," Ross piped up.

"If you know something, you *will* tell me," Charlotte said through gritted teeth.

"Shut up, Ross," Grandpa said. "I done told ya digging for 'seng so close to them fancy-pancy houses were beggin' fer trouble, and I was right." He turned his back on Ross. "We heard some terrible screaming one day, and it ain't been sittin' right on my conscience, neither."

Charlotte swallowed hard. Sure, she was aware of the methods traffickers used to break down their captives, but she'd kept that knowledge tucked away in a don't-go-there zone. Now it was all she could think about. Jenny was one of the screamers. And jackasses like Linton and Ross heard them and did nothing to stop it.

"When?" James pressed.

"It's been since we found that patch last week. At first, I thought I was a-hearin' thangs, but several days passed, there weren't no mistakin' that a girl was screaming. Spooked me. We hightailed it outta there, and 'bout five minutes later, a shot was fired."

"But did you actually see anything?" Charlotte asked. "If we had a witness—"

Grandpa shook his head so hard that his beard whipped from side to side. "No, ma'am. We ain't seen nothin'."

"What about you?" James asked Ross.

"I ain't seen nothin'."

Charlotte sighed and gestured for James to follow. About six feet away from the men, she stopped by a copse of pines. "I'm surprised Sammy didn't hear the shots and drive over." She kept her voice low.

"He heard and radioed me. I told him to stay put, thinking these guys might have been hired to provide a distraction while the kidnappers transferred the captives out. If I'd known you were in danger…"

She waved a hand in dismissal. "I've handled worse. So how are we going to transport these two to the station?"

"Sammy's already taken care of it. A cruiser should be on the main path any minute."

Whew. She'd had enough exercise for the day without having a mile trek to James's cabin with two fugitives in tow. "Junior will be glad to hear it. He's been whimpering like a baby ever since I stomped that knife out of his hands."

Oops. Mistake to bring that up. James's jaw clenched again, and she sensed the anger seething from his entire body. "Old man give you any trouble?" she asked quickly. "I kept expecting to hear his shotgun fire."

"Nah, once he saw the writing on the wall, he gave it up quick. Sorry. I should have chased the younger one. Would have if I'd known he had a weapon."

"That shouldn't enter into your decision. We're partners—equals." She held up the bag. "How much is this stuff worth?"

"You can fetch anywhere from five hundred to a thousand bucks a pound for wild ginseng."

She whistled and glanced down at the strange-looking plants. "You're joking, right?"

"'Fraid not. They've been poached so much it's possible they'll become extinct in a few years."

What a damn shame.

"What's so magical about ginseng?" she asked.

"People claim it can cure anything from cancer to diabetes to weight loss."

James regarded the poachers, rubbing his chin. "Forget your occasional murderer preying on lone hikers walking the trail. Between the moonshiners, pot farmers and 'sengers, Appalachia can be a dangerous place. Atlanta's crime rate has got nothing on us."

"And now you've even got human trafficking."

"Not for long," he vowed. "Not on my mountain."

Chapter Ten

James settled into a chair in Harlan's office. The hot seat, judging by Harlan's scowl. That, and the fact his boss had told him to come alone and leave "that woman" behind, clued him in that this wasn't going to be a pleasant conversation. James mentally reviewed the ginseng poacher arrests he'd made yesterday with Charlotte. Everything had proceeded smoothly. This had to be about the trafficking case. Harlan leaned back and ran a hand through his hair.

"What's up?" James asked.

"I've just spoken to the mayor. There's been a backlash from our questioning at Falling Rock. Numerous complaints and a formal petition for the mayor to 'do something about me.'"

"Rich folks' complaints. We've done nothing wrong and the mayor knows it. Did Madeline Stowers and her husband lead the charge on the petition?"

"He didn't mention any names, but it wouldn't surprise me."

He'd be lousy at Harlan's job and the ensuing political pressure that came with holding a public position. Mostly he'd hate the necessary kowtowing to the rich and powerful that came with an elected office. But James had enough sense to realize his resentment of the upper echelon was partly a result of his own upbringing as a Tedder. People had always judged him by the black sheep in his family and it had left him with a huge chip—no, make that a *boulder*—to carry.

"Surely he understood the necessity for questioning everyone," James said.

"He did—but he's still not happy about the situation."

Anger flushed the back of James's neck. "Maybe the mayor should be more concerned about the safety of his officers and the welfare of the people in his city than he is with keeping up an all-is-well appearance about crime in the area."

"Was that little speech for my benefit, too?" Harlan asked brusquely. "Because if it was, I can assure you that I have my priorities straight."

He said nothing. Let Harlan make of it what he wanted. Bad enough to have this tension at work, but the fact that this man was his brother-in-law might make the next family get-together awfully awkward.

"I've been reviewing my conversation with Captain Burkhart, Charlotte's supervisor. Her claim that the traffickers operate here stems from an unreliable witness."

"But don't forget that she saw a young girl at the window."

"Exactly. *She* saw it—not you."

Heat lanced his gut. "You accusing her of being a liar?"

"Not deliberately. Hell, James, sometimes people are so determined to prove a theory that they actually invent things in their own mind as proof and believe it's real. Detective Helms has admitted to a personal involvement in the case and that's always dangerous. It can cloud your judgment."

Harlan was nothing if not stubborn. "What about the men who tried to run us off the road? You can't blame that on a figment of imagination."

"No. But it's possible the incident had nothing to do with covering up a human trafficking ring."

"What else could it be?"

"Let me put it to you this way," Harlan said slowly. "Ever since you found that woman in your cabin, trouble has followed. We know something is going on, but is it really what she claims it is? I'm concerned about Detective Helms's mental health."

James jumped to his feet. "Like hell you are. You're concerned about not making waves with the mayor and the Falling Rock residents."

"That's not fair," Harlan snapped.

A voice sounded from the doorway. "I can assure you, Sheriff, that I'm not unhinged. Although I'm not sure how one goes about proving their own sanity."

Charlotte leaned against the door, face washed of emotion. It was as though she'd donned a professional mask of indifference. But Harlan's words had to cut her deeply.

"You don't have to prove anything," James said hotly.

"Sorry you overheard it this way," Harlan apologized. He turned to James. "I'm afraid she does have to set my mind at ease. I can't risk your safety, or any of my other officers' safety, unless I'm convinced there's good cause."

"Can you give me until the night of the fund-raiser to prove my case?" Charlotte asked. "Just a few more days."

He nodded stiffly. "Sounds fair. In return, I ask that any inquiry you make into the alleged trafficking ring is done discreetly. This office can't afford to alienate the mayor and a significant portion of the people we're here to serve."

"Understood."

With that terse word, Charlotte turned on her heel and left.

Tension clouded the air between him and his boss. "May I be excused?" James asked.

Harlan waved a hand toward the door. "You two have until this Sunday to find enough proof of the trafficking to obtain a subpoena, or better yet, get this matter resolved."

"You've made that very clear." James strode to the doorway.

"Wait a minute. James...don't let your emotions blind you to the facts."

"Don't worry yourself on my account. And don't you let the bigwigs dictate what your office can and should investigate."

He retreated before Harlan could whip out another angry retort.

THE RIDE HOME had been tense and quiet. "I don't want to talk about it" was all Charlotte would say about the matter.

He stirred the camp stew and took the cornbread from the oven.

"I'm glad you know how to cook," she commented, setting out the plates and silverware. "Because I sure don't."

"You can thank Lilah. She always cooks more

than enough for her family and then sends me the frozen leftovers."

"She's too good for Harlan." Charlotte clasped a hand over her mouth. "Oops. Didn't mean to say that out loud."

"Harlan's okay. We used to be best friends in high school. The two of us and Sammy used to go hunting and camping almost every weekend during deer and duck season. We did our share of sipping moonshine together under the Appalachian moon."

"Sounds like a real manly bonding experience. Did it bother you when he married your sister?"

"Took a little getting used to." He set the stew on the table. "Did feel strange at first when I got back from my tour of duty."

"And he offered you a job working for him?"

He returned to the kitchen for the cornbread as Charlotte ladled the stew into their bowls. "Yeah. Not sure how much of that was Lilah's doing, or whether or not he really needed me."

"You're a good cop. He's lucky to have you. Do you like the work?"

"Surprisingly, yes. Solving cases is like putting together the pieces of a puzzle."

A smile curled her lips. "I see you haven't had time to get jaded yet."

"The army already did that for me." His cell

phone vibrated, signaling a text message. He picked it up from the table and swiped the screen.

Back off.

What the hell? The phone number didn't ring a bell. He'd run a check on it tomorrow, but odds were that it was generated from a burner phone.

"Problem?" she asked.

"Nothing to worry about." He turned off the phone and laid it down. What good would it do to tell her of the vague threat? And he certainly didn't plan on mentioning it to Harlan, either. He'd only point out that Charlotte might have sent it, or that the threat could be about anything and not necessarily the trafficking case.

"I have to admit this is nice." Charlotte bit into a piece of buttered cornbread and then took a sip of sassafras tea. Her knee injury was almost completely healed. Luckily she enjoyed the tea's strong, tangy flavor and dutifully drank a glass or two a day.

"What's nice?"

"Being able to relax in the evening and have dinner with a friend. Usually I grab fast food, when I remember to eat, and scarf it down in front of the TV."

Friend? To hell with that. He wanted to sleep with her the night through and wake up with her every morning in his bed. Images of her spread on his couch in T-shirt and panties the night he'd tended her wound interrupted his train of thought. What had she just said? Something about food. He cleared his throat.

"I can relate. If not for Lilah, I'd never get a home-cooked meal."

"Ribs still hurt?" He'd insisted on X-rays and was relieved to discover none of her ribs were broken.

"Not too bad. The bruising looks worse than it feels."

He reached for the butter at the same moment as Charlotte. Their fingers touched. Heat traveled up his arm like an electrical charge—hard, fast and almost painful. He'd tried to be hands-off, but these nights alone with her had taken their toll. Everything she did and said drew him deeper into her spell.

She jerked her hand away from his as if the contact had burned. Charlotte felt the fire, too. He read it in the spots of color staining her cheeks, in the sharp inhalation of her breath. James reached for her hand and held fast. Her gaze moved slowly up from their clasped hands until her teal eyes, darkened to the color of the forest, bore into his own.

"Charlotte," he breathed. His heart skittered as if he'd run a race for his very life. He pushed back his chair. Wordlessly she rose from the table and came to him, never breaking their handhold.

IT WAS AS if every ounce of her considerable willpower had flown the coop. She dropped into his lap, pressing her hands into the top of his shoulders.

And then he kissed her.

His tongue danced inside her mouth and she was drowning in a flood of desire. She needed him—all of him. His fingers raked through her hair and then pressed into her scalp, drawing their mouths even closer. His desire pressed against her left hip. James stood and his hands cupped her ass, pressing her more intimately into his erection.

"Wait. Stop." She withdrew from his kiss and took a deep breath. "This is too fast…"

He let go immediately, leaving her dazed and disoriented, as if she'd lost her mooring. Charlotte grasped the edge of the table behind her for balance.

James ran a hand through his hair. "If you're not ready, okay. I thought…"

"It's not that I don't want you," she quickly assured him. "It's just… I don't want you to think it changes anything. No matter what happens at the fund-raiser, by this time next week I'm back in Atlanta."

A momentary flash of some emotion—pain? Sadness?—swept across his normally stoic features. "I get that. But it's not like Atlanta's on the other side of the country. We could visit."

"No. You don't understand." How could she make him see? "Being undercover is nothing like a regular job with regular hours. If you visited my place at the wrong time, you could jeopardize my cover."

"So? I'll call first or we could meet elsewhere."

Charlotte stepped away from his intense scrutiny and paced the kitchen. "There's more. Sometimes an assignment requires me to be away for weeks at a time. That's why undercover officers hardly ever have intimate relationships. Or if they do, it rarely lasts."

"We could try," he insisted.

Damn, James was stubborn. She threw up her hands, exasperated. "Don't you get it? I'd be terrible for you, for any man. Harlan's right—trouble follows me. I never know when some ex-con with revenge on his mind might find me."

He held up a hand, warding off her objections. "I'm willing to tolerate a little inconvenience. And as far as danger, I can handle it, so stop borrowing trouble. We can take this one day at a time."

"Are you sure?" She anxiously searched his face. He deserved more than what she had to offer. He deserved a Lavender Mountain woman who could spend her evenings with him, share these cozy meals and be there to listen as he unwound at night and talked about his day.

She was not that woman.

"You're an all-or-nothing kind of man, James. With strong views about right and wrong. I don't want to hurt you."

"Let me worry about my own feelings." He crooked a finger and gave a lopsided grin. "I'm a big boy and can take of myself. Trust me?"

Like no one else. He'd never abandon her when danger went down, unlike Danny. And James cared about her.

She slowly walked toward him, drawn to his strength and to her body's urgent need to feel him inside her. To know him intimately. His hands rested on either side of her hips and he kissed her forehead, his lips tender and warm.

The tenderness completely undid her. Some small knot of reserve deep inside melted. Charlotte buried her head against his chest and shuddered.

"You alright?" he asked gruffly.

His voice rumbled against her cheek, the vibration setting off a corresponding rumble in her heart and a seismic shift in her soul. This wouldn't do. *"One day at a time,"* he'd said. For tonight, she'd find pleasure in his arms and not analyze her feelings. The trick was to focus on the physical, to imagine this as a temporary fling.

Charlotte raised her chin and found his mouth, eagerly succumbing to the passion. She pressed her body against his so hard that the table slid against the wall. He groaned, and the knowledge of his need fueled her own even more.

His hands were everywhere at once, down her back, against her ass, then roaming up the sides of her ribs toward her breasts. All while his lips trailed kisses down her neck and to the hollow of her throat. Impatiently she tugged at his belt. Without missing a beat, James undid the buckle and she pushed down his uniform pants.

He groaned again—or wait—was that her? Or both of them? Didn't matter. She cupped his most intimate parts and felt the velvet steel of his erection. "I need you. Now."

"Not yet."

He suckled her nipples and inserted a finger into her core. When had he removed her pants? Her fevered brain hadn't noticed anything but the unbearable throbbing at the apex of her thighs, the need to be joined. "Now. Please," she whimpered against his mouth.

"Hell, yeah," he growled. "You're so hot and ready for me."

He took her hand, evidently intending to lead

her to the bedroom. But that would take way—way—*way* too long. She couldn't, wouldn't, wait. Charlotte shook her head. "Here. Now."

"If you're sure you really—"

She smothered his mouth with kisses and wrapped her arms around his neck.

As if she weighed nothing, James hoisted her legs around his hips and flipped their positions so that she was seated on top of the table. He entered her quickly and she met his thrusts with an increasing urgency.

Harder, harder, harder...faster, faster, faster. Her body tensed and then exploded with pleasure and release. The muscles on James's back tightened and spasmed beneath her hands as he reached his own orgasm.

His head sank onto her shoulders and the sound of their labored breathing joined together. Her fingers gently traced lazy circles down his sides.

"I think I need to sleep," she said with amusement. "About ten hours or so."

He laughed and swept her into his arms. "I don't know about sleeping, but I'm all for going to bed early and often. No more sleeping in the guest bedroom for you." He waggled his brows.

Charlotte returned his grin, feeling more relaxed and carefree than she had since Tanya had called two weeks ago saying that Jenny was missing. "Lucky for you—" she began.

An angry buzz vibrated the tabletop.

"Not again." He stared at it, frowning.

"Better answer. It could be work."

"It is." He let her down and she hastily pulled her clothes together.

"Officer Tedder," he said. A moment's pause. "Okay, we're on our way."

Hope fluttered in her chest. "Any news on the traffickers?"

"Nope. Domestic disturbance."

"No one else is available?" Resentment quickly spoiled her afterglow, followed by the familiar weight of guilt. It was her own fault the sheriff's office was stretched thin.

"The surveillance at Falling Rock leaves us shorthanded. This shouldn't take long; the disturbance is just a small piece down the road."

Amusement tugged his lips as he surveyed the spilled camp stew that ran off the table and puddled on the floor. "This will be a mess to clean up later."

Charlotte put her hands on her hips and arched a brow. "Are you complaining?"

"No, ma'am. I wouldn't change what happened between us, even if it means staying up all night scrubbing floors."

His lopsided grin made her breath catch. Who

was she kidding by thinking that sex with James could be a mere physical fling? That her life and heart could continue on same as before?

Tonight had changed everything.

Chapter Eleven

Blue strobe lights flashed across the night landscape, illuminating a disheveled clapboard house that had enough junk lying around the yard and porch to stock a small store. James hopped out of the car and headed for the door. "Stay behind me," he ordered.

Charlotte shot him the dagger look. "Like hell I will. And next time it's my turn to drive."

So much for postcoital afterglow. It was back to business as usual.

Screams reverberated off the house walls.

"You cheatin' sack of—"

"—crazy heifer. Put that poker down or I'll—"

"—who is she? I'll kill you first and then I'll kill her."

James shook his head. "I believe we can ascertain the root of the argument here. Which was no doubt enhanced by shots of moonshine." Idly he wondered if it might be some old batch of 'shine his father and uncle had produced. The irony of that never escaped his notice.

"You been called to this house before?"

"No, but these domestic disputes are amazingly similar."

Charlotte kicked an old tricycle out of her path. "Voluminous consumption of alcohol and a short fuse by one or both partners?"

"Followed by a cooling off period and teary reconciliation until the next round of drinks. You got it. Remember, these types of calls can turn out to be the most dangerous."

"Even undercover cops know that," she said, voice brusque.

James pulled open the screen and wrapped on the door. "Sheriff's office. Open up."

"See what you done did, woman?" a man shouted from inside.

"What I did? What *I* did? You stupid, lying—"

James turned the knob and discovered it was unlocked. He entered and took in the scene at once.

A heavyset woman in a floral print dress brandished a poker in her right hand. The man wore only a pair of boxers. Blood ran down his nose and he swayed slightly, off balance. But James's focus quickly passed the couple arguing and traveled to the couch where two young girls—

probably ages four and five—huddled together beneath a Hello Kitty blanket.

"Ma'am, put down the poker," he said firmly. "Let's discuss this calmly."

"Ain't nothin' to discuss. I told him to git out and he won't leave."

"This is my house," the man bellowed. "You go."

James caught a movement from the corner of his eye—Charlotte reaching for her firearm. He flicked his wrist downward, motioning her to put it away. She raised a brow, hand hovering over the sidearm, but nodded and dropped her hand to her side.

"I'm ordering you to drop that weapon," James said, stepping between the two.

The woman lowered her gaze and stared at the poker blankly, as if she'd forgotten she held it. Her face was flushed and her eyes wild with rage.

Charlotte also stepped between the couple, facing the man and spreading her arms out wide. Together, the two of them provided a visual and physical barrier between the couple.

"There we go," James said, his voice softer. He stepped closer and took the poker from her shaking hands. "That's better. Could you do me a favor, please?"

"What the hell do you want? I ain't done talking to him yet." She tried to walk around him and James blocked her path.

"Ma'am, see your kids over there on the couch?" he asked. "Maybe it'd be a good idea to take them to their bedroom. You don't want them to witness this. You're a good mom and know this isn't good—"

"It's his fault," she muttered. "Pulls my chain every time."

"Officer Hanson, could you go with her and the kids? Sir, I need to you take a seat over there." He pointed to the recliner across from the sofa.

The man did as told, and Charlotte walked to the children, giving them an encouraging smile. "Everything's going to be alright. Your mom's going to tuck you in bed. Good deal?"

The youngest girl clutched her doll tighter and regarded Charlotte with solemn eyes that belied her age. The older one asked her mom, "You want us to go?"

The mother pursed her lips into a tight line and faced Charlotte. "I want him gone, ya hear?"

"We'll discuss that later," Charlotte said. She bent her knees and came eye-level with the youngest girl. "Such a pretty doll. What's her name?"

"Emily."

"Nice. What's your name?"

"Sarah Slackum. I'm four years old and live at 19 Pence Street." Sarah smiled at her mom. "I 'membered, Mama."

The woman teared up. "Ya done good, honey. Said everything like I told ya to do if'n ya was lost or the police asked ya questions."

James kept his focus on the man as the women left the room. "What happened here? Did she hit you in the face with that poker?"

"Damn sure did." He grasped the arms of the recliner and held tight.

The man had the nervous energy of an angry, caged tiger. He still needed to be talked down a few notches.

"How did this get started?"

"I come home late and she started accusing me of being with another woman. I've had it up to here." He karate chopped the air by his neck.

"Been drinking?" James nodded at the mason jar of applejack moonshine on the coffee table.

"A wee bit," he admitted. "But so did Edna."

"You need to go to the hospital?"

"Nah. This ain't nothin'."

"You want to press charges?"

The man snorted. "I'd hear no end of that at

the factory. Everyone would make fun of me getting whupped by a woman."

"This a regular occurrence with you and your wife?"

"This ain't the first time," he admitted. "Ought to be in yer records somewhere about us."

"It's not good for the children. Ever considered getting counseling?"

"I ain't no alcoholic."

"That may or may not be. But I'm suggesting that you and your wife take anger management classes."

"But she hit *me*. Edna's the one that needs them there classes."

"Think about it for your children's sake. I'm reporting this domestic disturbance to a social worker. She'll talk to you and your wife about the classes and check out the children's safety. Be expecting a visit."

"What's he still doin' here?" Edna cried out, striding toward them.

Charlotte blocked her path and ordered her to sit on the couch. Surprisingly, Edna complied, putting her head in her hands. Her whole body shook with sobs.

"You'll be glad to know your husband isn't pressing assault charges," James said.

Edna dropped her hands and snapped her face up. "But it was his—"

James held up a hand. "You can't assault people. Ever. For now, let's just try to get through this evening without this situation escalating. Think of your children."

Silence at last descended in the room.

"For tonight, I think it's a good idea if you two are separated. Have either of you got somewhere you can go for a night?"

"I ain't a-leavin' my children," Edna said. "Make Boone go."

Boone rose. "Didn't plan on stayin' here's no way. I'm staying with Grady." He grabbed a jacket and weaved his way outside of the house.

James followed him onto the porch. "How do you plan to get there? You can't drive anywhere in your condition."

Boone held up a cell phone. "I'm callin' my brother to come git me."

"We could give you a lift."

"Nah, Grady be here in less than five minutes. I'll wait here on the porch for him."

THEY WATCHED AS Boone climbed into his brother's pickup.

"Great job in there," she said, leaning her head back in the car seat. "Nice touch about contacting the social worker."

James nodded and started the cruiser. "I'll make sure either life gets more peaceful in that house, or the children are removed if they're in danger."

She cast a sideways glance, studying his strong profile. He'd be a great father one day—calm but firm, and loving. Tonight's call had been tense, but they'd worked together as a team, and every time she saw James in action, her respect for the man grew.

"I see how your department is a real asset to the community," she observed thoughtfully. Normally she measured success by the number of arrests made and the amount of contraband recovered. But there was another side of law enforcement, too. One where officers worked with more normal citizens and aided the vulnerable who needed them to intervene on their behalf.

"We try. The job has turned out to be a lot more enjoyable and interesting than I imagined it would be."

"What made you take it to begin with?"

"I was drifting after getting out of the army. Had become a bit of a recluse, actually. Then the opportunity came along and I took the job, thinking it would be easy, steady work."

"Must have been difficult reacclimating to civilian life after leaving the army."

"A little," he admitted. "I wanted peace and quiet when I returned home."

"Pretty rough over there?"

"I've seen and heard things that no man can easily forget. Ended up with a mild case of PTSD." He shot her an uneasy glance. "As my partner, I probably should have mentioned that to you sooner."

"I trust you, and evidently Harlan does, as well."

"Overall, I'm grateful for my experience in the army. It's defined who I am."

And he was a damn fine man—if a little bossy.

He might claim the job was coincidental, but there was more to it than that. "I don't believe you went into law enforcement only because it was convenient. You went in because you believe in justice, especially considering what's happened to your family."

He slanted her a thoughtful look. "Maybe. Glad to know I have your trust. I have a feeling you don't trust others easily."

"I don't." She drew a deep breath. What had Miss Glory said about opening her heart? James had opened his a crack, she could do the same. "My partner before you, Danny, ran out on me during a botched drug bust. Left me alone with a pretty scary suspect who had pulled a gun on us."

"What a son of a bitch."

"It gets worse. We...had a thing going for several weeks before this happened." There. She'd spit it out. What a fool she'd been.

"A double betrayal," he said, mouth grim. "That explains a lot."

The police radio crackled. "Fire reported at 101 County Road 14. Fire truck en route. Nearest officer please respond."

Charlotte rolled her eyes. "Is there a full moon tonight?"

"What the..." James picked up the mike. "Officers en route."

"Can't someone else take this call?" she asked. "We've done enough—"

"That's my cabin." He flipped on the blue lights and siren, hit the accelerator and spun the cruiser onto the road.

Charlotte held on to the door pull. "Your cabin," she repeated slowly. Coincidence? No. That old place had been standing for decades. This was a message.

She licked her suddenly dry lips. Guilt weighted her shoulders. She'd brought this on James.

They raced through the darkness in silence. Did he blame her for his old homestead going up in flames?

Her phone vibrated in her pocket and she pulled it out.

This is just the start.

Damn. The anonymous text left no room for doubt. The fire had been intentionally set. Charlotte slipped the cell phone back into her jacket pocket without comment. She'd tell James about it later. He had enough on his mind at the moment.

In record time, James pulled the cruiser onto the cabin property. At least a dozen other vehicles were parked helter-skelter in the yard and spectators had already gathered, watching as firefighters sprayed giant hoses on the inferno. Orange flames toasted the black sky and the fire's roar muffled the murmur of human voices.

There was no saving the family cabin. There wasn't even the possibility of saving any items inside, though she doubted anything of sentimental value had been left behind. Anger blazed inside her, as hot as the wall of heat emanating from the burning building. The perpetrators were probably long gone—if this was a professional job orchestrated by Maddie. If so, the bitch was probably standing at the window of her plush mansion, watching as fire glow lit the woods below.

But if the arson was a mere crime of opportunity by a pervert…her gaze drifted to the tree line. He could be hiding behind one of those trees, getting off watching the sight of his work. She glanced at James, but his focus was all on the cabin. His hands were on his hips, his face stoic. She longed to touch him, offer words of sympathy, but that would hardly do in public. Besides, she'd be of more use to him by finding the perp.

Charlotte slipped into the crowd and then hurried around to the back of the cabin. Only one lone firefighter fought the flames from the opposite direction. She jogged toward the woods, right hand resting on the holster of her gun.

A crash boomed from behind and she whirled around. The left cabin sidewall collapsed to the ground and the roof sank on top of it, shooting sparks like the Fourth of July. The smell of burnt pine stung her eyes and enveloped her nose and lungs. She swiped at her eyes and continued into the woods.

Leaves, twigs and pine needles crunched underfoot, loud as firecrackers in the sudden stillness. Only a few feet past the tree line and the noise of the fire and firefighters was already muffled.

Screech.

Her stomach cartwheeled and she raised her gun, spinning in a circle to discover where and what had sounded. Blood pounded in her temples.

And again, the cacophony arose. *Whoo whoo.* "Just...just a barred owl," she whispered.

Creepy thing was loud as a foghorn. "Nothing to fear."

But it took several seconds before her heart ceased its rapid pounding and her breathing returned to normal. Charlotte lowered her gun and searched the inky blackness for signs of anyone hiding.

Nothing was out of the ordinary. Barren tree limbs reached skyward and the tops of shrubs were laced with crisscrossed shadows from moonbeams. The wind whispered above and around her.

So why was she so sure that she wasn't alone?

Awareness prickled her scalp and snaked down her spine. Someone watched. She listened and strained to pinpoint a location.

"Charlotte? Charlotte? Are you out there?"

James. She exhaled in a whoosh and cautiously stepped forward.

Twigs snapped like a mini explosion from her left side. Footfalls vibrated the ground and at last she could make out the tall figure of a man running deeper into the woods.

"Halt," she called out.

The man kept running, just as she'd expected.

"Charlotte? Everything okay?"

"I'm fine," she reassured him. "Be right out."

She stepped out of the forest and quirked a brow at his stern face. "I was checking to see if our arsonist was watching all the excitement."

"Without backup? What were you thinking?"

His dad's cabin was in flames, so she bit off an angry retort. He had enough on his plate without her reminders that he wasn't her protector on the job. "You were busy," she said mildly. "Any leads about what started the fire?"

"They won't say yet but we both know what happened here. Especially since…" He clamped his mouth shut.

"Especially since what?"

"I wasn't going to mention it but I had a text last night saying to back off."

She shook her head in disgust. "Why didn't you tell me?"

"Didn't seem important. I mean, c'mon, it changes nothing. Neither of us will ever back down from pursuing this."

She marched past him, eager to leave the dark shadow of the woods and whoever had been out there hiding. "You still should have told me. If you were working with Sammy, I bet you would have, right?"

"Maybe," he agreed, falling into step beside her. "And don't think I'm finished. Promise me you won't run off on your own again without at least telling me what you're doing. That's professional courtesy at the very least."

"I can admit when I'm wrong. Sorry. I won't do it again."

"Excellent. I take it you didn't see anyone?"

Charlotte hesitated, but she could hardly with-hold information after she'd just chastised him for doing the same. "There was someone out there, but he took off running and I never saw his face."

"You could have been…" He broke off his chain of thought. "Never mind. You're here and safe."

"I had a text, too, on the way over. It said, 'This is just the start.'"

"The Stowerses are getting desperate and they know we're the ones investigating."

"I wonder how much else they know."

They trudged back to the fire, wrapped in their own thoughts.

The fire wasn't quite as bright and the flames were lower. It wouldn't take much longer before the firefighters had it completely extinguished.

"Sorry about your dad's cabin."

James shrugged. "Maybe it's all for the best. The place was a hard sell for buyers and neither Lilah nor I had any desire to move in."

"Speaking of Lilah, I see she and Harlan are here."

"And she's brought Ellie. At least you'll get to meet my niece."

The little family headed toward them. Lilah appeared solemn, but the toddler at her hip was clearly entranced by the fire, and stared at it with saucer-wide eyes.

"Hey, Ellie," James said, holding out his arms.

Charlotte ran a hand down Ellie's blond curls. "Such a pretty girl."

Ellie graced her with a cherubic smile before turning her attention back to James. "See the fire, Uncle Jim Bob," she squealed.

Charlotte snickered.

He winced. "Uncle James," he corrected her mildly, taking Ellie into his arms. "You okay, Lilah?"

She nodded, but her lips trembled slightly. "Yeah. A little sad, though. Me, you and Darla had some good times there."

They watched in silence as the hoses continued to beat down the flames. Most of the spectators drifted away, driving off in their vehicles. Harlan put an arm around Lilah's shoulder. "No point hanging around," he said quietly. "The cold air can't be good for Ellie's cold."

"You're probably right," she agreed.

They all walked together to Harlan's car and James strapped Ellie into her car seat.

"Sorry about the cabin," she said to Lilah.

Lilah wasn't her usual vivacious self, but she mustered a tight smile. "It represented our past. And it held as many painful memories as good ones. As for me, I'll keep my focus on the present."

Harlan glanced significantly at James. "Like I said—trouble," he muttered.

Resentment sliced through Charlotte, but she said nothing in protest. How could she? Harlan was right. She'd brought nothing but trouble to James.

Soon, she reminded herself, this would all be over. She'd leave Lavender Mountain and leave James. In time, he'd forget her and move on with his life—as would she. The thought should have been comforting, but it filled her with sadness.

Harlan dug into his jacket pocket. "I'd been on the way over to your house to deliver this." He held out a certified letter. "Captain Burkhart called me and said to make sure to find you. You've been formally summoned to a hearing to-morrow to discuss dismissal for job abandonment. Your suspension was over yesterday and you were supposed to have reported back to work today."

Damn. She hadn't paid any attention to the date. Atlanta seemed a lifetime ago. "Tomorrow," she repeated dully.

"We'll go together," James said, shooting Harlan a defiant look.

She stuffed the envelope into her pocket. "This isn't your problem."

"You're not going alone. End of argument."

Like hell it was.

Chapter Twelve

"The choice is yours. Report for work here tomorrow morning or be dismissed."

"I need more time," Charlotte pleaded. "Just a few more days and—"

"You're fired," Captain Burkhart said, smugness evident in his pronouncement.

She clamped her jaw shut and arranged her features to show no emotion. She wouldn't give him the satisfaction of knowing how those words hurt.

The man had never liked her. Whether it was because he was a sexist cop or because he'd taken offense for some other unknown reason, Charlotte couldn't say. But in the two years he'd been her supervisor, he'd made her job hell.

When she'd reported Danny and Roy's abandonment at the alley, he hadn't believed her. Instead he bought into her partners' lies that she'd been at fault for the life-threatening danger with the drug dealer. According to their false version of the story, she'd carelessly blown their cover and then fled the scene. Valiant men that they were, her partners claimed they stayed behind and pursued the drug dealer—at great risk to their lives.

Charlotte shook off the old memories and fought for composure. The two other detectives at the hearing stared at her with a modicum of sympathy.

She rose and lifted her chin. "I used my suspension to pursue this case. My only fault is checking back in a day late. The punishment's a little stiff for the offense. All I'm asking is permission to use my annual leave for the next few days."

Burkhart slapped his hands on the desk. "Enough. We've been through this. You're insubordinate and I don't believe you ever intend to return to duty."

"Not until I have my arrests," she agreed.

"And now you'll never get one." He also rose from behind his desk. "You no longer have any authority as a police officer. Turn in your badge on the way out."

She bit the inside of her mouth, not wanting to lash out and set him straight. She might no longer be employed by the Atlanta PD, but Harlan could still deputize her to work in his jurisdiction until she'd arrested the Stowerses. Right now, she couldn't think about her future career. All that mattered was rescuing Jenny. After that, she'd have to come to grips with the mess.

"Richard and Maddie Stowers will be arrested by the end of the week. You can count on it," she promised.

Burkhart's face reddened. "Not by you. Let it go, Helms."

Hell, no. Easy for him to say. He didn't have a personal connection to the case. Nor did he have to interview trafficking victims and hear the pain in their voices and the horror in their eyes. She couldn't save everyone, but she could and would save Jenny.

She snatched up her purse and marched to the exit, slamming the door behind her. James was sprawled on a bench in the hallway. For the first time, she was secretly glad he'd insisted on accompanying her on the trip to Atlanta.

He quirked a brow. "Bad news, I take it?"

"I want out of here." The institutional-green walls and gray linoleum flooring, combined with the faint scent of industrial cleaner mixed with sweat and tobacco, were a sudden anathema.

"Couldn't agree with you more."

He matched her step for step as they left the building and climbed into her car. She turned on the engine and they headed into the late afternoon traffic.

"I'd hate to drive this every day," he observed from the passenger side.

She cast him a wry smile. "We're not even in rush hour traffic. Sure you don't want to drive like usual?"

"Nope. It's all yours."

Well, at least she'd won that battle today. Wordlessly she weaved along the crowded interstate, stewing over the long day spent at the hearing.

James interrupted her thoughts. "You can always appeal their decision, you know."

"And go through another kangaroo court?" She laughed dispiritedly. "Six years of stellar service—all down the drain on my first transgression."

"Sounds pretty stiff. You should fight it, or at least file a complaint about the severity of the judgment."

"Maybe." But she couldn't muster enthusiasm for the task. When had she stopped loving her job? It had happened so gradually. "I used to enjoy working undercover," she said. "It was exciting and it felt like I was making a difference. Stupid, huh? For everyone I arrested, it seemed like three more criminals replaced them by the next week."

"Would have been even worse on the streets if you didn't catch the ones you did."

"I suppose. But I get sick of the whole underground culture, too. And not getting to see my family as often as I want."

"Now you're free."

"Now I'm broke." A sudden worry assaulted her. "You really think Harlan will temporarily deputize me until the end of the week?"

He winked. "He's my brother-in-law, so I have some influence. Lilah could make life hell for him if he didn't help us out on this. Besides, you're a great cop and he knows it."

The words were a balm to her injured pride. Much as she'd grown to hate her job, she'd never been fired before, and the idea rankled. Maybe James was right. She should file a complaint and get her employment record cleaned up from this hit. Plus, it would have the added benefit of irking Captain Burkhart—always a plus.

It took forty minutes to drive the ten miles to her apartment, but at last she pulled into the parking lot and they headed up the stairs. While she was nearby, it'd be crazy not to pick up more street clothes, a fancy gown for the fund-raiser event and a few other little odds and ends.

They climbed the concrete stairwell and she dug the keys from her purse. A strong hand rested on her forearm. "What—?"

James frowned and cocked his head at the

slightly ajar door. "You leave it unlocked?" he asked in a low voice.

She felt the blood drain from her face. "Maybe the landlord had to get in." Not likely.

James drew his gun and stepped in front of her. "I'll check it out."

"Not alone you won't."

He shot her an irate look. "Just stay back."

She unholstered her own sidearm and tried to squeeze her body in front of his. "Me first. It's my apartment and I know the layout better than you," she argued.

James muscled her behind him and slowly opened the door.

Books and sofa cushions littered the den floor. Every item on her bookshelf had been dumped and furniture was pulled away from the walls. James took a step in and she followed, her eyes sweeping from the kitchen to the dining room and balcony. The same mayhem from ransacking was everywhere, but no one was in sight.

That left the bedroom and two bathrooms to check. She carefully picked her way through the junk on the floor, sliding past James. He wasn't happy about that, but could hardly argue the point.

The hall bathroom was empty, all the contents of her medicine cabinet toppled into the sink. Which left the bedroom—the only room where lights weren't blazing. An unnatural still-ness lifted the hairs at the back of her neck. If someone was in there, they knew she'd returned. She flattened herself against one side of the door, and James joined her on the other. She was about to enter, when he beat her to the punch.

He kicked the door and it slammed against the far wall. Charlotte flipped on the light switch.

Two men dressed head to toe in black, their faces hidden under dark ski masks, erupted from the closet. The two barreled toward them, so quickly she barely had time to catch her breath—much less shoot. One of the men chopped her arm holding the gun, and her weapon hit the floor by her feet. Strong arms grabbed her just above both elbows and then violently threw her to the side. She was airborne for two seconds before rolling clear across the bed. Her forehead smacked the bedpost and pain radiated through her head. Warm liquid trickled into her eyes and she swiped at them, seeking James in the melee.

Her attacker had fled, but James was wres-tling on the floor with the other man. She had to help him. She located her gun and tucked it back into her holster.

"Go get the other guy," James grunted.

"No way."

"I got this," he insisted.

The need to help James warred with her need

to catch the other intruder. They'd violated her sacred space. Every nightmare come true. If she didn't catch the fleeing felon, she would always worry that he would return one night. And the next time she might not be lucky enough to have a partner by her side.

"Be right back," she promised, racing to the stairwell.

The steps were slick with rain and she lost her footing, tumbling down the first flight. Ignoring the burning shinbone scrapes, Charlotte ran on and scanned the back of the property.

A silhouette in black crouched behind a garbage can. At first sight of her, the intruder took off running again, knocking over the dumpster can, spewing trash everywhere. But she was close enough—in shooting range—if her aim was accurate. Charlotte touched the gun she'd slipped back into her holster. *You aren't officially a cop anymore. You shoot the guy and you've got a mess on your hands.*

The moment's hesitation cost her a chance. He reached the street, blending with traffic and pedestrians.

She bent over, hands on knees, and took deep breaths that burned her chest. *Get it together. James might need you.* Charlotte straightened and ran back upstairs, ignoring the jabbing stitch in her side.

PAUSING TO REASON with Charlotte had cost him the advantage in the fight. The masked man fought with the desperation of a cornered animal. Trying to wrestle him back down was like trying to bathe an angry wildcat.

"Who the hell are you?" James panted as they rolled on the floor.

No answer.

The scent of sweat and cheap aftershave filled his nostrils and lungs. He fought against the downward spiral that might tunnel into another flashback. *Keep it together.*

Pain seared his left thigh as the man landed a vicious kick.

Had he momentarily blanked out and weakened his hold? James groaned and grabbed one of the attacker's feet, trying to prevent another kick. Where was Charlotte? Fear pinched his gut. What if this guy's accomplice stopped running and went on the attack? To hell with this wrestling match. Charlotte's safety was his priority.

But he could accomplish one important victory—get a good look at who was behind the attack. If he was lucky, he'd find this criminal later. James released his grip and reached for the knit ski mask, ripping it off his face.

Startled gray eyes met his. James soaked in every detail possible—cropped brown hair, ruddy complexion, a hawk nose, thin lips. His gaze dropped lower and hit the jackpot—on the right side of his neck was a dagger tattoo. The mark looked to be a crude prison job with its lack of detail and grayish-black coloring.

The guy rushed the doorway and James gave chase. Halfway down the stairs, he spotted Charlotte coming toward them—alone and seemingly intact, but blood trickled down her face. Relief chased down his neck and spine. The man she'd been chasing was nowhere in sight, but she was now in the direct path of the gray eyes.

"Look out," he shouted.

Too late. The intruder never slowed, but he raised one muscled arm and knocked her out of his way. In horror, James saw her petite body absorb the pounding of concrete until she lay motionless at the bottom of the stairwell.

"Charlotte!" He rushed to her prone body and pushed the hair from her face. In the space of mere minutes, hell had unleashed its fury. She was pale, the whiteness contrasting with the crimson ribbons of blood on her face.

She groaned. "You okay? Did they get away?"

"Yes, on both counts. How bad are you hurt? I don't want to lift you if anything's broken."

She struggled up onto one elbow and drew several shuddering breaths. "I think I'm okay. Give me a minute."

"That's one nasty cut above your left eye." He

pulled a handkerchief from his jacket and gently dabbed at the open wound.

She flinched and reached for his arm. "Stop. I'm going to try to stand."

He supported her weight on one side of his body and she sagged against him. "This is officially the worst day of my life," she joked. "Lose my job and then get the crap beat out of me. Now I get to return to my destroyed apartment and pick up the mess."

"Leave it. I'll lock up while you wait in the car. Where's the nearest hospital? You need stitches."

"I won't argue with you this time. We can stop at a doc-in-the-box on our way back to Lavender Mountain."

James quickly locked up her apartment. Slowly, they returned to the cruiser, his arm bracing her around the waist. "Think you might have sustained internal injuries?" he asked anxiously. Each time pain flickered in her green eyes, he sank lower into guilt. At last they reached the car and he carefully tucked her inside before entering it on the opposite side.

James keyed the engine and turned up the heat. Charlotte leaned back in the seat and flipped the mirror down. "Holy crap, I'm a mess. I promise I don't feel as bad as I look."

She faced him. "So what's wrong?"

"What's wrong? Everything. You're hurt and it's my fault."

"Don't say that." She pointed to the cut on her forehead. "That was caused by an unknown assailant. Not you."

"Yeah, an assailant who escaped me."

"We were surprised by an attack and neither one of us is to blame. I noticed you were limping. What happened?"

"Bastard landed a lucky kick." He gripped the steering wheel and stared out into the rainy darkness.

A warm, soft touch on his right hand startled him, and he glanced down. Charlotte's small hand caressed his tense fingers, which were white at the knuckles.

"I'm okay," she whispered, her breath clouding the air. "Those men did enough of a number on us without us piling on and beating ourselves up."

"Back there. I might have lost it for a couple of seconds in the fight," he admitted. "I'm not sure."

"Doesn't matter. My mind was a tilt-a-whirl a good thirty seconds after I crashed into the bedpost. As they say, shit happens. All we can do is our best."

But what if his best wasn't good enough? Some small part deep inside still felt broken from the war. It was getting better—much better—in large part because the insomnia had finally been laid to rest. The past nights he'd spent with Charlotte in his arms, he'd drifted into deep slumber. James loosened his grip from the steering wheel and held her hand, staring at their enjoined fingers. Every word, every touch from Charlotte was a balm to his spirit—that is, when they weren't arguing. A smile curled his lips. Fussing with Charlotte was still more fun and invigorating than normal conversation with anyone else.

The rain came down harder, a metallic din that thundered above and around them. Water washed across the car windows in sheets. It seemed as though they were separated from the rest of the world in a warm, safe cocoon.

Her hand traveled up his arm, and even through the jacket, the contact set his heart pounding as loud as the rain outside. She brushed her mouth across the edge of his bottom lip. "There's no need to hurry back. Let's wait out the storm together."

He kissed the top of her scalp. "If you're sure the stitches can wait."

"Kiss me and I'll forget all about the cut."

"I aim to please." His mouth met hers. What he'd intended as a tender gesture escalated at once into a roaring desire and he pulled away. "Not the time or place," he said with a frustrated laugh.

"Tonight, then."

The promise and passion in her eyes wiped away all pain and all misgivings. Somehow, someway, they belonged together.

Chapter Thirteen

The last three days before the Stowerses' fund-raiser event sped by way too fast. She and James spent most of their days outlining their plan of action for rescuing Jenny, and their nights...well, she'd never been happier. It was going to hurt like hell to return to her dreary apartment in Atlanta once this case was over. There was nothing there for her—no job, no lover and no friends. Her undercover work had consumed all her energy for far too long.

Charlotte checked the cruiser's pull-down mirror and smoothed back the few stray locks that escaped the bun on the back of her head. Her dyed ebony locks had faded a bit from repeated washings, and the gallon of conditioner she'd used had helped the damage, but it was still a disaster. The stitches above her left eye were removed yesterday, but no amount of makeup could cover the nasty bruise.

James laid a hand on the top of her bare shoulders. "You look beautiful," he assured her.

She smoothed a hand across the long green evening gown, thankful that its length would cover all her shinbone scrapes. Sure, she was being vain and embarrassed that James guessed her trivial concern. Crisply she closed the mirror and raised the sunshield flap to its original position. "Doesn't matter what I look like—all that matters is finding Jenny. And you look pretty spiffy yourself, by the way."

Did he ever. He filled out the tuxedo like nobody's business. The suit emphasized his lean, muscular build and lent an elegance to his high cheekbones and strong jaw. Her admiration must have been clear because his eyes darkened and his gaze shifted to her lips.

"Don't you dare kiss me," she warned.

Teasing mischief danced in his eyes. "Afraid you'll need to have me right here and right now if I do?"

"No, I just don't want you to ruin my lipstick."

"Liar."

She knew what he was trying to do—lighten the tension before they entered the Stowerses' mansion.

"Good thing our plan doesn't include having to actually dance. That bruise on your thigh looks rough."

Music spilled from the main level of the Falling Rock Community Clubhouse and every window was lit. It appeared so elegant and enchanting—if one weren't aware of the dark underside that funded such privileged wealth. If she had her way tonight, the Stowerses would spend the rest of their years in a dark, damp cell with no music. And even that wouldn't atone for all the lives they'd ruined. *I'll have Jenny home to you by dawn*, she silently promised Tanya.

James lifted her hand and kissed the inside of her palm. "We'll find Jenny and the others," he promised. "We've got our plans in place."

"Right." She inhaled deeply.

"One more thing."

She gazed once more at the glittering clubhouse, a hand reaching for the door, impatient to get started.

James placed a finger under her chin and gently turned her face to his. "I love you."

"Wh-what?" No, oh no. This wasn't supposed to happen. She'd let him get too close.

"You heard me. Does that really surprise you? I thought after last night..."

She swallowed hard. Last night had been magical. There'd been a certain tenderness along with the passion, emotions that she didn't want to examine at the moment.

"Don't love me," she whispered. The hurt in

his eyes matched the hurt in her heart. "I bring trouble to everyone. Can't you see that?"

"I've told you before that I don't care. We can face anything together." He sighed and ran a hand through his hair. "Never mind. I shouldn't have brought it up now."

"You'll always be special to me...the best friend I ever had."

Friend? The word crushed his spirit. He wanted it to be so much more than that.

"James..." Tears threatened to ruin her carefully made-up face, and she couldn't control the tremble in her lips.

"Sorry. Really. You don't have to say anything." He cleared his throat. "Is your mike secured?"

Relieved to get the conversation back to the job at hand, she checked to make sure it was safely tucked into the front of the low-cut gown. "Yes. Ready when you are."

He nodded and opened the car door. "Showtime."

The wind chilled her bare skin and she hastily threw the gown's matching wrap over her shoulders.

They walked side by side to the front door, mingling with several other couples also on their way to the party. Everyone else looked excited and happy to be going to the annual fund-raising event, while a hard knot of misery twisted her stomach. She'd hurt James and she'd never meant to do so. He deserved a woman who would fill his life with good things—not her.

The door opened and they entered into the bright warmth. A live band played classical music that underscored the chattering of the houseful of guests.

Her eyes quickly swept the room of beautiful people dressed in formal attire. Serving staff milled about with glasses of champagne and shrimp canapés. She'd thought the Stowerses' house beautiful, but it was nothing compared to the present festive glory of the clubhouse.

"Thank you for joining us." Maddie appeared in the foyer dressed in a red low-cut gown that managed to be bold yet flattering. She ignored Charlotte and extended a hand to James. "Officer Tedder, if I remember correctly? Richard and I appreciate all you do in keeping peace and order in our community."

Yeah, I bet she appreciates us. Phony witch.

"I believe y'all are the last of the officers to arrive," Maddie said, still avoiding Charlotte. "Harlan said everyone's made it here except for one officer left manning the fort and another who's home sick."

That would be Sammy, who was guarding the

back of the place, and Charlotte wouldn't be surprised if the Stowerses were aware of that fact.

"I don't believe you've met my husband before?" Maddie swept her hand toward the man at her side, who gulped a healthy swig of bourbon from a crystal glass.

Richard Stowers glanced Charlotte's way and discreetly looked her body over. But not so discreetly that it escaped her attention. A cheesy smile lit his puffy, albeit handsome, face, and he extended a hand. "And you must be Officer Tedder's wife?"

"Partner. Officer Hanson." She masked her displeasure at his handshake, which he held two seconds longer than customary.

His eyes narrowed in on her forehead. "Nasty cut you have there. What happened?"

As if he didn't know. As if the two of them hadn't sent those men to search her apartment for clues on how much she knew about their trafficking ring. Unless…unless Maddie were the brains behind everything while he merely enjoyed the fruits of her ill-gotten gains. Richard certainly didn't look or act the part of a criminal mastermind. His ruddy complexion, and the web of broken veins around his nose, suggested he either imbibed quite frequently or was an alcoholic.

His remark finally drew Maddie's attention

her way. Brown eyes flashed at her, barely able to disguise anger.

Charlotte offered a cool smile to Richard. "I took a tumble down a flight of concrete stairs."

"Ouch. Guess it could have been worse, though," he said jovially.

Maddie's sharp chin jutted out even further than normal. "Colleen," she said peremptorily, summoning her housekeeper, who apparently served double duty at social functions. "Please take their jackets." Maddie faced them both with a chilly smile. "Enjoy your evening. Let's move along, Richard."

Charlotte removed her wrap, uncomfortably aware of Richard ogling the low-cut V of her gown before obediently tagging along behind his wife.

"Your purse, ma'am?" Colleen held out her hand.

She firmly pulled the sequin purse closer to her side. "I prefer to keep it with me, thank you."

Richard sidled up close to Charlotte and she drew back an inch. Annoyance stiffened her spine. The last thing she needed was to have this man clinging to her side while she searched his house.

James took her arm and guided her away. "Excuse us. We'd like to catch up to our friends by the buffet."

"Certainly." Richard took her other hand and pressed it into his coarse palm. "See you in a bit. Perhaps a dance later?"

Not if she spotted him first. Next time she saw Richard, she vowed it would be to handcuff the creep.

"Of course," she lied, accompanying James into the den, where a long buffet table was spread out the length of the entire room. Once they were out of earshot she quickly whispered, "Thanks for helping me escape."

James nodded. "I see my sister and Harlan. We'll talk a bit and then…"

Then, they implemented their plan. She nodded in silent agreement. With any luck, Richard would be too drunk to seek her out by the time they began the house search.

"Champagne, ma'am?" She accepted a slender flute from the waiter. He was tall and stocky and clearly uncomfortable in his ill-fitted uniform. No doubt he was also employed as a guard, same as the Stowerses' supposed gardeners. She exchanged a knowing glance with James.

"Be careful," he muttered.

The man just couldn't help himself when it came to unnecessary warnings. "Don't worry about me. I can take care of myself. Focus on your own—"

"Look at you all spiffed up in a tux!" Lilah

rushed over and hugged James. "I haven't seen you in one of these since your high school prom." Her gaze swept to Charlotte and she clasped her hands in admiration. "Stunning."

"As are you," Charlotte said. Lilah's long blond hair was loose and she wore a lavender tea-length dress. But even more striking was her happy confidence. You'd think she'd grown up attending swanky parties every weekend. But as for Harlan…she stifled a grin. He tugged at his collar and looked as if he wanted to be anywhere but here.

Lilah's gaze fell to Charlotte's feet and she let out an exasperated *tsk*. "Too bad I couldn't talk you into high heels, or at least wedge pumps."

As if she'd attempt smuggling out Jenny and the other girls while tottering in high heels. She caught Harlan's warning glance—Lilah was in the dark about tonight's mission. Just as well. Let her have her fairy-castle, enchanting illusion for the evening. The less people that knew, the better their chance for success.

The band came to an abrupt halt.

"May I have your attention, please?"

Maddie and Richard posed in front of the band, and her cultured voice swept over the crowd. Conversations halted.

"As everyone is aware, we've gathered here tonight to honor our sheriff, Harlan Sampson, and all of the men and women employed by the Elmore County Sheriff's Department."

Richard raised his glass in the air. "Hear, hear!" he called out a tad too loudly.

Maddie slanted him a look.

"Bet she gives him hell later," James murmured by her ear.

"Not if they're locked in separate cells."

He clinked his champagne glass against hers and smirked. "Hear, hear."

Maddie continued. "It's because of their hard work and dedication that the Lavender Mountain community is such a peaceful haven."

A smattering of applause broke out.

"And now I'd like to ask Sheriff Sampson to come forward and say a few words."

"Damn," Harlan muttered.

"Speech," Lilah said with a grin, giving him a playful shove forward.

Now was the time to slip away. "I'm going to the ladies' room. Be back in a bit," Charlotte lied.

"Wait until after Harlan's speech and I'll go with you," Lilah offered.

"Sorry. It can't wait."

She cast a last look at James. His face was stoic, but she knew he hated her operating alone. Yet they'd both agreed beforehand that it would be less conspicuous if they searched apart from one another. She gave him a reassuring smile and strolled toward the side exit of the clubhouse, all while casually sipping the flute of champagne.

At the rear of the main ballroom she stopped at the buffet table and picked up a canapé, using the opportunity to check if she were being watched. Luckily all eyes appeared focused on Harlan's clipped speech. She dabbed at her mouth with a paper napkin and then whisked out of the room and into a back hallway with an exit door.

One last furtive glance behind, and Charlotte slipped outdoors. Cool wind whipped through the thin material of her evening gown and she shivered, thinking longingly of her jacket. But soon enough, she'd be back inside. On the sidewalk, she passed a couple decked out in their finery, obviously out of town guests on the way to the party. The woman's voice was a tad too loud and the man practically carried her as she stumbled about in her high heels.

Charlotte waved at them cheerily. "Forgot my lipstick," she said. "See you in a bit at the party. The band's fantastic."

"Oh, damn." The woman placed a hand over her mouth. "I believe I forgot mine, too. I'm going back, Thomas."

Thomas rolled his eyes. "You look fine. Let's go."

Charlotte beamed at him, practically bestowing

a conspiratorial wink. "You go on. Me and—" She glanced at the woman.

"Alyssa," she supplied. "Alyssa Renfroe."

"Alyssa and I will go in together and meet you in a few minutes."

"You sure?" he asked doubtfully.

"No problem."

He transferred the weight of Alyssa to Charlotte's arm, and she fought to keep her balance while propping up Alyssa. Their progression to the Stowerses' house was slow and arduous, but Charlotte was grateful for Alyssa. What a struck of luck. Now she didn't have to sneak into the house. Alyssa had unwittingly provided an alibi.

Once at the Stowerses' entrance, Charlotte didn't bother knocking and opened the door like she had every right to be there.

A tall, husky man entered the foyer and gave them the once-over.

"We forgot our… What did we forget?" Alyssa asked with a giggle.

"Lipstick." Charlotte smiled at the man and kept walking. "I'm staying in the east wing. Are you?" she asked Alyssa.

Her smooth forehead puckered. "I—I'm not sure."

"Don't worry. We'll find your room."

It took several minutes to make it down the hallway, but at last Alyssa came to a halt. "This is it," she declared. "I recognize my perfume bottles on the dresser."

"Great. My room's further down. I'll be back in a few minutes," Charlotte lied, relieved to be rid of her drunken burden.

She'd been down this particular hallway on her previous visit with James and didn't expect Jenny or the others to be kept so close to the party. But for the sake of thoroughness, they'd leave no room unexamined.

Every bedroom off the hallway was presently empty, but appeared to be used as a guest bedroom for the weekend. Each contained luggage, clothes hung in the closets and a few toiletries were set on the nightstands. Charlotte peeked out of the last room she'd entered to make sure the coast was clear before stepping back into the hallway.

"So sorry you are feelin' poorly, ma'am," Colleen said in her distinctive Irish accent as Charlotte started to enter the den.

Charlotte ducked back inside the nearest bedroom and flattened herself against the wall.

"Let me help you find your room," Colleen continued. "This way, please, ma'am."

She let out a deep breath and listened to the women make their way down the hall. Time to slip away.

Charlotte scurried out of the room, still clutching the small sequined purse that was just large enough to hold her cell phone and a small gun. The hallway made an L-turn and she ventured on, but it was more of the same—empty rooms.

Until she entered the last room on the right.

Someone was in there. A mattress squeaked and a man and woman groaned. Uh-oh. Hastily she backed out and softly shut the door. Had they heard her?

She waited a few heartbeats, prepared to make a lame excuse if they came after her, but the mattress squeaks never slowed.

Whew, bullet dodged. Charlotte retrieved her cell phone and texted James.

East wing complete. Negative. No need to break in. Go inside and say your name is Thomas Renfroe and you are checking on your wife, Alyssa, who returned for some lipstick.

A rough hand grasped her elbow. "What the hell are you doing here?"

THE BAND RESUMED playing and James waited several minutes before strolling through the crowd, biding his time until he had an opportunity to leave unnoticed. A teenage girl clutched the arms of an older gentleman and her gray eyes were wide and…not exactly scared, but apprehensive.

Was the man her father or one of the Stowerses' clients? He needed to check the west wing of the Stowerses' house and then find Charlotte—the quicker the better. But he couldn't ignore the girl, either. He turned and scanned the crowd for Harlan.

His brother-in-law was surrounded by people congratulating him on his speech, but as if he had an extra sense for danger, Harlan raised his head and made eye contact. James cocked his head at the old-man-young-girl couple and Harlan nodded in understanding. He'd check it out.

"Look at her," a lady said close by. "Never thought I'd see a Tedder at an event like this."

Another voice murmured assent. "Heard Sampson's hired her brother now."

"Harlan's in bed with the dregs of our community," another chimed in. "Disgraceful."

Heat fevered his brain. They could say what they wanted about him, but not his sister. She was off limits.

James squared his shoulders and eyed the small clique. "Lilah Tedder is one of the kindest, smartest women you'll ever meet. Harlan's lucky to have her for a wife." He focused his gaze on the sole male among the group. "And if you've got a problem with me, let's discuss it now."

"No problem," the man said quickly. "Ladies, let's head to the buffet table for refreshments."

They made a quick beeline to move away and James took a deep breath. He shouldn't have confronted them. The last thing he needed was to make a scene. Their plan depended on acting as unobtrusive as possible. He meandered out of the room, relieved nobody paid him any mind. At the back door of the clubhouse, he exited onto the deck. No one was around. Quickly he walked through the backyard. If someone asked what he was doing, he'd claim he needed fresh air.

His cell phone vibrated and he read the text message. Great. Charlotte was safe. Soon as he finished searching the west wing, they were to meet by the kitchen.

Sure enough, he easily got past the man monitoring the front door. The moment he was alone, James began his search, going into every room— a couple of bedrooms and baths, a fully equipped gymnasium including a sauna and a movie theater room.

The hallway was eerily quiet. The Stowerses had excellent acoustics in their place. Perhaps they'd built the mansion that way to contain the screams of desperate children. His pace picked up. No way he'd leave this place without every room searched. If Jenny was here, they'd find her.

His spirits sank with each empty room. But the most likely place the girls were hidden would be either on the upper level of rooms or in the basement. They'd expected this going in. James entered the den and searched for Charlotte. No luck. She might already be hanging around the kitchen area. He hurried to the door—but still no Charlotte. Stealthily he opened the door several inches, but the room was dark and quiet.

No Charlotte.

Unease tingled at the back of his neck. Where was she? He pulled out his phone and checked the time the text was sent—five minutes ago. She should be here.

He pushed away from the kitchen and reached for his phone. A familiar smell of roses startled him. "Charlotte?" He whirled around.

"The one and only." Her voice was light but her expression subtly strained.

"Where were you?" he whispered fiercely. "What happened?"

"One of the male serving staff grabbed me and asked what I was doing in that area. I tried to play it off as if I were lost and looking for the bathroom, but he wasn't buying it."

He stood between her and the doors, half expecting security to arrive and escort them out of the house. Or worse. "How did you get away?"

"I acted all embarrassed and haltingly admitted that I'd gone there in search of my married lover. Claimed we'd made a rendezvous, but I couldn't remember which room we were supposed to sneak into. Then I put on my best snooty air and said that Maddie and Richard were close personal friends and if he didn't leave me alone I'd have to report him."

"Quick thinking. Guess you learned it on the job."

"Sink or swim, as they say." She shivered and rubbed her arms. "I'm okay. Let's get on with it. We don't want to draw attention to ourselves in case guards are lurking about."

"Agreed." He kept his voice low as they walked by the pantry. "Kitchen appears normal but we can take another quick peek before heading upstairs."

"I want to see as much as possible before we search the attic and basement. Make sure no child is left behind when the raid begins."

People liked to tease him about his military rigidity, but Charlotte was just as thorough in her job process.

What a shame this gorgeous house was owned by such a despicable couple. How many years had the Stowerses managed to conceal their illegal activity and live this lifestyle?

A deep voice suddenly boomed from around the corner. "Did you see that drunk chick—Alice or something—stumbling around the house?"

"Her boobs were practically hanging out of her dress," another man replied, chuckling.

Quickly James took Charlotte's hand and they ducked into a side room as the men made their way past.

"That was close," she breathed at his side as they slowly eased their way back into the hallway and proceeded to the staircase. Sneaking upstairs would be even trickier than the basement. Anyone passing through the foyer would see them. Timing was everything.

A quick look back and then they bounded up the stairs together. Again, he was struck by the unnatural quiet as they left the den and walked the hallway. As mapped out earlier, he searched the rooms on the right while Charlotte worked the left. They made quick work of it. He glanced in the last empty room on his side and joined Charlotte for her last search.

A heavy padlock hanging on the outside door set him on edge. Even if it wasn't locked now— why was it ever necessary to lock someone inside?

Half a dozen cheap cots lined a stark room that was unlike the opulence of the rest of the living quarters. The beds were meticulously tidy, even though they were made up with only threadbare sheets and blankets. He entered and shut the door behind him while Charlotte flipped on the light.

A scratched armoire was the only other piece of furniture besides the cots, and Charlotte flicked it open. A few lone wire hangers dangled from the top dowel, but it was otherwise empty.

"Could be the maid's quarters," he said quietly.

"This isn't the Victorian era where indentured servants were forced to live in substandard hidey-holes."

She walked to the lone, narrow window and pulled back the tattered curtain. "And then there's this," she whispered.

He ran a finger down the pane's tinted liner. "Bingo."

Charlotte's eyes grew misty. "They're gone. Sold. I'm too late."

"There's still the basement." But his own spirits grew low.

The scrape of a shoe sounded far down the hall. With unspoken accord, they rushed to the door and positioned themselves on either side, backs flat against the wall. Charlotte flipped off the light switch.

A crescent moon struggled to shine through the tinted and curtained window.

Creak. Another step closer.

James hardly dared to breath, concentrating on the patterns of sound.

Creak, creak. Just one person. He carefully extracted the gun from his vest and closed his finger on the trigger, the metal cool and lethal in his hands. A rustle of movement beside him, and Charlotte extracted a gun from her beaded purse. Her face was pale but composed in the faint light.

A flashlight beam crisscrossed on the floor outside their door. He was closer now. With any luck, the man was only on a routine security check.

The footsteps reached the end of the hallway and stopped.

Silence as thick as the stale, dark air weighted down on him. He noted the rise and fall of Charlotte's chest, although she made no sound. What was the man doing on the other side of the door? James gave her a slight nod. *Be ready for anything*, he silently willed her with his mind.

The world exploded in a firestorm of splintered wood as the man kicked down the door and entered. The scent of sweat and cheap aftershave stabbed through the chaos of his mind. *The intruder at Charlotte's apartment.*

A metallic clatter ripped through the darkness, like the sound of automatic gunfire in Afghanistan. James shook off the memory. *Not now. Stay in the moment.* His eyes focused and he realized that Charlotte had knocked the gun out of the man's hand. That noise had only been the sound of it harmlessly hitting the floor.

The man raised a fist to her, ready to strike.

James lowered the boom. Raising his arms high, he thrust downward with his gun and knocked the guy on the back of the head. He never saw it coming and crumpled to the ground with a heavy thud.

"Go get some pillowcases and blankets," he told Charlotte, kneeling beside the injured guard. Handcuffs were in his pocket, but the first order of business was to gag the intruder. One loud yell and their gig was up. James rolled him flat on his back. Had he killed the guy?

He moaned. James hastily grabbed the sheet from Charlotte, rolled it into a cylinder and gagged him. "Get another sheet and tie his feet while I cuff his hands."

They worked quickly, and all the while he strained to listen for more footsteps. So far, so good.

"Here." Charlotte pressed the intruder's flashlight into his hands. "We might need it."

Curious, James flicked it on and shone it on the man's face, glancing at the dagger tattoo on his neck. Gray eyes glared back, defiant to the end.

"Got you now," James said with grim satisfaction.

Charlotte tugged at his tux sleeve. "Let's go find Jenny."

Chapter Fourteen

Charlotte gathered up the hem of her long gown and checked the hallway before entering.

Behind her, James spoke softly into his mike, filling Harlan in on their progress. "Bound suspect upstairs, heading to basement. Any news?"

Charlotte held her breath. What if they'd been spotted entering upstairs? Harlan might call off the whole mission if Maddie was breathing down his neck.

James winced. "Ten-four."

"Well?" she asked.

"Sammy hasn't seen any activity out back and the gate officer reported no young females have exited Falling Rock. We're on."

"So what's the bad news? I saw that look on your face."

"The usual. He says abandon the mission and don't attempt a rescue if there's more than one guard down there. And call backup if needed."

Charlotte bit her lip, hoping for James's sake

there wasn't more than one guard so that he wouldn't have to break Harlan's orders. Secretly she and James had agreed to take on two guards if necessary.

And in her heart of hearts, Charlotte made her own secret vow. She wouldn't jeopardize James's life if there were three or more guards—but she'd return alone and attempt a solo rescue operation, despite all the odds against success.

At the end of the hallway, James suddenly pulled her in for an embrace and gave her a quick, fierce kiss. "Be safe," he ordered.

Love and worry blazed from his blue-hot eyes. It took her breath away. But before she could even process her thoughts, James stepped around her and surveyed the area. "We're clear."

Together they hurried down the stairs. In the foyer, she pressed his hand. "Good luck."

This is where they parted ways again.

She hurried past the kitchen and started by the main entrance.

According to the architectural drawing, there was another entrance to the basement behind the main level utility room, third door past the kitchen. She swept inside and locked the utility room door behind her. To the right of the washer and dryer was yet another door. Quickly Charlotte hurried over and gave the knob a turn.

Locked. Of course it was.

She opened her purse and extracted the tiny pick and tension wrench that both fit in the palm of one hand. She and James had practiced for this eventuality, and he'd been taken aback at her skill. This wasn't her first time to pick a lock.

Assured no one was about to witness the break-in, Charlotte set to work inserting the wrench into the bottom of the keyhole and the pick at the top of the lock. She scrubbed the pick back and forth. A little twist here and there and—*ping*—the metallic click fell into place. She turned the knob and cracked the door open.

"—getting hungry," she heard a deep voice say. "We should go upstairs and filch some of their alcohol."

"Hell, no. Maddie would have a fit. Ain't worth it."

Damn, there were two guards at least. She listened harder, praying a third voice didn't chime in.

"Stop acting like a wuss. She won't know. Don't need two of us to guard one door. Them bitches are locked up tight. They ain't goin' no-where."

A smile curled her lips. She wasn't too late. Jenny and the other girls were so very, very close. She and James had a shot at making this work. Charlotte dropped the wrench and pick in her purse and texted James on her cell phone.

I'm in. Only two guards. Girls locked in storage room inside basement.

Setting her purse behind the dryer, she lifted out her gun. It took all her self-control not to rush in with her gun blazing and demand their release. But she and James had a plan. For now— she waited.

JAMES RETURNED HIS cell phone to his pocket with a sigh of relief. That had taken a little longer than anticipated. On his end, the basement entrance door hadn't been locked so he'd already deduced that if the girls were downstairs, they were locked in one of the two storage rooms. If he were the Stowerses, he'd have taken those extra precautions.

Taking a deep breath, he threw open the door and stomped down the narrow stairs. "Halloo," he called out, slurring his voice. "Where's da bathroom?" he asked, belching loudly. "I need to—"

"Hey, you can't be down here," a man quickly answered.

"Whaddaya mean by that?"

A burly guy appeared at the bottom of the steps. "No guests allowed down here."

"That's b-b-bullshit." James staggered and

clutched the handrail, as if he were too drunk to keep his balance.

"Sir, you have to go. Now."

With satisfaction, he watched the guard start up the stairs. "But, but I—I'm Richard's pal." James fell on his rear end and stumbled down two steps. He let go of the rail and waved his hands in the air. "Whoa. Them stairs are st-steep."

The guard scowled, climbed up to him, and grabbed his arm. "You have to—"

With all his strength, James pulled the guard down with both arms. The man gaped in surprise and James landed a swift punch to his gut before the guard regained his senses and realized what was happening.

The man doubled over in pain but had the presence of mind to keep his arms locked around James. Together, they tumbled down the stairs. James's mike and cell phone clattered to the ground.

"Hey, what's going on?" he heard another male voice shout.

Excruciating pain suddenly radiated from his right shoulder. The son of a bitch had bitten him. James kneed the man in the groin and the pain eased as the man stopped biting and let out a strangled yelp.

"What the hell?" the other guard shouted.

James saw him reach for a gun that was belted at his waist. Where was Charlotte? Right about now would be a good time for her to make an appearance.

From his position on the floor at the bottom of the stairwell, he spied her flat green shoes and a swatch of green fabric advancing toward them. His avenging angel in emerald. He strained his neck upward and watched as she pushed her gun into the second guard's back.

"Drop your weapon," she demanded in a hard voice.

"Who? What? Ah, damn it." The guard bent his knees and placed his weapon on the ground. Charlotte kicked at the gun and it spun several feet across the concrete floor, out of grabbing reach.

James rolled his prisoner onto his stomach and jerked one of his hands behind his back. "Sheriff's office. Don't resist arrest. You'll only make matters worse for yourself."

"Okay, okay," he groaned. "Don't hurt me."

He made short work of slapping on the cuffs. "Say one word and you're dead," he warned before leaping to his feet. "You, too," he told the other guard.

Charlotte spoke, nudging her pistol into the suspect's back. "Get on the ground spread-eagle, hands out in front."

He complied without a word of complaint, and James quickly cuffed him.

"We need more gags," Charlotte whispered.

"We'll make do." He tore off his tie and gagged one of the prostrate men on the floor.

Charlotte glanced down, running her hands down her hips over the sleek gown and frowned. "I don't have anything... Wait." She raised her hands and tugged at the velvet ribbon holding the bun at the top of her hair. Her hair cascaded down and she held the ribbon in front of her, eyeing it critically. "Not as strong as I'd like, but it will do."

"Give it to me," he said.

"Get the storage key from him first."

James grabbed the man's chin. "Where's the key?"

"You won't get away with this," he grunted. "Guards are everywhere patrolling the grounds. Let me go and I'll cooperate."

Charlotte knelt beside him. "We don't need your cooperation, Ricky—that is your name, isn't it? You're the one who shot at me."

James patted down the man's pockets. "Nothing here."

Charlotte turned to the other prisoner. "I'll pat him down."

James pulled the ribbon tight between his

fists, holding it in front of the guard's face. "Last chance to talk."

"Okay, okay," Ricky said, breathing hard. "But remember I cooperated later if I get arrested."

James said nothing, advancing the gag toward his mouth. There'd be no deals for scumbags like Ricky. He wanted everyone involved in the trafficking business to get the stiffest sentence possible.

"It's in my right shoe."

James exchanged a bemused glance with Charlotte, and then untied the man's sneaker and shoved it off his foot.

A small brass key dropped on the concrete.

Charlotte snatched it up with a trembling hand and they stared at one another, disheveled and breathing hard. "We did it," she whispered. Her green eyes shone with tears.

Bittersweetness gnawed at his heart. He loved Charlotte's strength and courage, but even more he loved her vulnerability and fierce loyalty. She might not love him, but he'd stood beside her when no one else would believe or help in her quest to rescue Jenny. That would count for something in Charlotte's book, and he'd take what he could get.

He took her hand and helped her to her feet. "Only one thing left to do."

She nodded and ran a hand through her hair.

"Right. I just…should be prepared for whatever we find behind that locked door. It'll be an ugly sight."

"Maybe it won't be too bad," he said gently. "After all, they want these girls to look pretty for their clients."

Anger crackled in her eyes and she lifted her chin. "That's not happening again. Let's go finish our job."

Chapter Fifteen

Charlotte held her breath as she turned the key in the lock.

"Wait." James's hand held her back. "Could be a trap or another guard waiting. I'll go first."

She shook off his hand. "We'll go in together." Before he could argue further, she thrust the door open.

The room was almost pitch black, with only a faint trickle of light from a high, small window. The stale, moldy scent of damp air assaulted her nose. Her eyes adjusted to the darkness and she saw the faint, pale outline of three young girls huddled together in a back corner. Groping along the concrete wall, she located the light switch and flipped it on.

The large, square block room was devoid of anything except the girls and a half-dozen cots with thin mattresses. James drew his gun and circled the middle of the basement for any hidden surprises.

"Don't shoot us," one of the girls screamed. "We've been good."

"Don't scream. Nobody's going to hurt you. I promise." Charlotte approached them slowly as James put away his weapon. She blinked at the unexpected sight.

The girls were gussied up to look like living Barbie dolls. They wore bright-colored, low-cut evening gowns, their hair was elaborately curled and styled, and their young faces were painted with red lipstick and heavy rouge. Their eyes were thickly lined in black kohl. In a gray room that held all the charm of a steel garbage can, they popped like discarded roses.

It took Charlotte several moments to realize the blonde in the middle was Jenny. She looked nothing like the last time she'd seen her with Tanya. Then she'd been fresh-faced, wearing blue jeans and a T-shirt, and sporting a wide, easy grin.

"Jenny. It's me—Charlotte. Your mom's been so worried about you."

Jenny hunched her thin shoulders and shrank back until she was pinned against the wall. "Don't tell her where you found me," she whispered.

"But, but…" Charlotte floundered, unsure how to proceed. This was hardly the grand welcome she'd expected.

A petite Asian girl with bobbed black hair eyed them warily. "Who sent you?"

James flashed his badge. "Sheriff's office. We're here to help you."

A whimper escaped the lips of the third girl, another blonde who appeared to only be about twelve years old.

Charlotte scrutinized the girl's features. She'd seen her photo listed in their book of missing children. "Lisa Burns?" she guessed.

Lisa's eyes grew even more terrified, but she left the other two girls and approached James and Charlotte on wobbly legs. "I'll do whatever you say."

"Hey, are y'all really cops?" the Asian girl asked. "Did you just come for Jenny?"

"We're here for *all* of you," Charlotte assured her.

The mistrust melted on her face and she ran to Charlotte, wrapping boney arms around her waist. "I want out. My name is Amy Chang."

"We'll get you out." Charlotte ran a hand over her smooth hair and eyed Jenny, who'd sunk onto a cot and curled into a ball. Leg cuffs bound her slim ankles.

"Promise?" Amy pulled away and swiped at her eyes. Mascara and liner ran down her face.

Lisa gasped and put a hand on her red lips. "You're all messed up now, Amy. They're gonna hurt you if we don't get outta here. We're supposed to be all pretty."

"Nobody's going to be hurt," James said. "You're safe with us."

"Safe?" Amy thrust out her right hand, wrist down. Deep scars crisscrossed the veins. "I almost killed myself six months ago. A few weeks ago, I got messed up one night, thinking crazy thoughts, and got scared I'd do it again. I called a teen suicide hotline. That's how I met Piper. She was so nice. Asked to meet me. Said she'd take care of me and keep me safe. I thought she was my friend." Amy's lower lip trembled.

Charlotte's heart squeezed until it ached.

"Stop it!" Lisa cried. "We're going to get in trouble. They'll come shoot us like they did Mandy when she tried to run away."

"Mandy?" Charlotte and James exchanged a look. The human blood on the leaves... That poor kid. She hadn't been as lucky as Karen.

"We should go," James said, casting a swift glance at the stairs.

Charlotte eyed the teary Lisa and recalcitrant Jenny. "Might be easier to call Harlan and have him come down here with backup."

"You still got your phone? Mine's probably busted."

"It's upstairs in my purse. I'll use my mike to contact Harlan."

"Good. Because mine fell in the tumble down the stairs."

Charlotte removed the small black disc tucked into her gown. "Officer Hanson to Sheriff Sampson."

Nothing. Not even a whisper of static. Charlotte blew into the mouthpiece. "Testing, testing."

"Damn it," James muttered. "I'll go search for my dropped phone under the stairs. There's an off-chance it's not smashed to smithereens."

Charlotte put a hand on Amy's and Lisa's shoulders, guiding them to the cot where Jenny lay. "Let's go talk to Jenny a minute."

They offered no resistance, as docile as lambs, and stood close by while she sat on the cot beside Jenny. Tentatively, Charlotte touched one of Jenny's delicate cuffed ankles. Besides being bound, she wore ridiculous sequined high heels. "Why the leg cuffs?" she asked. The others weren't cuffed.

"She tried to run away the first night," Amy volunteered. "She didn't even make it out of the house before they caught her."

Charlotte could only imagine the severe punishment for that defiance. No wonder she was so scared to try to escape again. "Jenny. Are you afraid to leave? You know me. I promise I won't let anyone hurt you."

Jenny's face was buried in a blanket and she vehemently shook her head. "No. I won't go."

"Why not?"

"Because." Sobs shook her body.

"Because why?"

Jenny suddenly sat up and faced her. "I've done…bad things with bad men."

"It's not your fault, sweetie."

"Yes, it is. I-I'm a bad girl. I ran away from home and then…they got me."

Charlotte wrapped her arms around Jenny and laid her cheek on the top of Jenny's head. "Shh. It's okay."

"But my mom… I don't want her to know."

"Tanya just wants you home. She misses you terribly and has been out of her mind with worry."

Jenny turned her head to the wall, refusing to listen. It was going to take lots of time and therapy to get this child over the brainwashing and abuse. And she'd been troubled to begin with. Tanya had finally admitted to her that Jenny had threatened suicide several times after her father had left home. But Charlotte didn't have time or therapist skills. Every second they spent in the basement meant the odds of rescue dramatically decreased.

Lisa suddenly screamed and cowered to the ground. Amy's mouth opened in horror. Charlotte's stomach cartwheeled as she jumped up from the cot and whirled around.

Footsteps creaked on the wooden stairs. Through the open step slats flashed a pair of shiny men's shoes and gray flannel pants. James heard it, too and ran to the stairs.

Richard Stowers stepped down and faced them, a gun drawn.

Charlotte blinked. This Richard was deadly sober. The affable albeit lecherous drunk from earlier at the party had transformed into a maleficent, hard column of a man whose eyes shone with a vicious intent. Or—more likely—this was no transformation, but an unmasking of his true self. The show of drunkenness might have been just that—an act to throw people off. It had certainly fooled her.

"Had a feeling I'd find you two down here," Richard said coolly. "Maddie might have underestimated y'all, but I didn't."

The utter calm of his voice was all the more terrifying for its unruffled focus. This was a man who could not be reasoned with or distracted.

James stepped in front of her and raised his gun. Charlotte maneuvered to his side. If they went down, they went down together.

"Drop it," Richard ordered.

"Hell, no. We appear to be at a standoff."

Amy let out a banshee wail that echoed in the

chamber like an explosion. Richard turned his head a fraction to determine the cause of the noise.

This was Charlotte's chance.

She dived toward Richard's knees. He stumbled backward half a step. Time slowed and her whole body attuned to every nuance of detail—

The stiff fabric of Richard's pants.

Amy's wails.

James shouting her name.

The thundering of her own heart in her ears.

A whoosh of air as Richard raised his arm.

His furious dark eyes intent on killing.

The cylindrical chamber of metal pointed at her head.

She'd always known it would come to this one day. But she didn't shut her eyes and she didn't regret her decision. Her mantra was always to see a job through to the end. No matter what.

Another swoosh of air and Richard was falling. Charlotte swiftly rolled toward the back wall. Richard's gun fired. An explosion of smoke and noise assaulted her senses—but no bullet ripped into her flesh. She was unharmed.

James jumped on top of Richard and landed a solid punch to the man's gut. The gun fell out of Richard's hand and she picked it up, scrambling to her feet. "Stop fighting, Richard. Or I'll shoot."

The men stilled and eyed her, Richard gaping in surprise, and James with a grin.

"No need for that," James said. "Stowers is going to play nice now." He grabbed an arm and twisted it behind Richard. "Roll onto your stomach and put your hands behind your back."

"Damn you both," Richard ground out harshly. "It's not over yet. Do you hear me? This is *my* house. And those bitches back there are mine, too."

Charlotte's anger rose to match his. "They aren't bitches and they don't belong to anybody."

James slapped the cuffs on Stowers's wrists.

Richard bent his knees and managed a sitting position. "They've already been bought and paid for. This isn't over yet. You'll never make it out of here with those whores."

"Shut your mouth," James warned, grabbing a fistful of the man's starched shirt. "Unless you want me to gag you like I did your guards."

Richard glowered but kept his mouth shut as James frisked him for weapons. He pulled out a cell phone from Richard's pocket and tossed it to Charlotte.

"Give me that back," Richard cried out. "You've no right to search my house like you did. When my lawyer's through with you— Hey!"

James pulled off the tie from around Stowerses' neck. "You had your chance."

Charlotte smiled grimly as James gagged the guy. Actually, the threat of his lawyers was a problem, but she'd cross that bridge later and she damn sure wasn't going to let the bastard know she was worried.

"I expect nothing but commendations from law enforcement for breaking this case," she boasted.

James stood and raised a brow at her. "After all, we did hear the victims cry for help when we entered the house to escort a guest to their room. I'd say that gave us a right to investigate."

Nothing but muffled curses escaped from Stowers's gag.

"Go on and take the girls upstairs and let Harlan knows what's happening," James said.

"But I can't get Jenny to agree to leave, and her feet are cuffed anyway."

"Then you go ahead and take the other two while I deal with Jenny. If I have to carry her out of here screaming, then that's what I'll do."

"Okay. Lisa, Amy, let's get out of here." Charlotte walked over to Jenny's cot and ran a hand through her blond hair. "Officer Tedder's going to carry you out. You can trust him, okay?"

Jenny's entire body started to shake. "No! Just leave me alone."

Charlotte dropped her hand and stared at her, unsure what to do.

James sank to his knees by Jenny and cocked his head toward the stairs, signaling for Charlotte to leave.

Taking Lisa and Amy by the hand, Charlotte ushered them across the basement. At the foot of the stairs, she glanced back once more.

James nodded. "I won't leave without Jenny," he promised.

And she believed him. He'd take a bullet before he broke that vow. Something fierce and warm and wonderful pulsed through her body. A feeling she'd never expected to happen again. She loved James. Loved and trusted him with a deep faith she hadn't imagined possible. She wanted to tell him, but now wasn't the right time or place. These girls desperately needed to get away.

"I know you will," she called out. Charlotte let go of Amy's and Lisa's hands. "I'll go first. Stay close to me and follow my orders."

The girls nodded in understanding, their eyes huge with fear.

They rapidly climbed the stairs. Each moment, Charlotte expected Maddie or one of her guards to appear at the open door. But the utility room was blessedly empty and she waved her hand at Amy and Lisa to follow her.

Charlotte gave them an encouraging smile, then turned toward the doorway and caught sight of her purse where she'd stashed it earlier behind the dryer. Quickly Charlotte dug out her phone and punched in Harlan's number.

They were so close to rescuing Jenny and the girls. All that was left was to find Harlan and get backup in place before arresting Maddie and Richard. Their guests were in for a real surprise tonight. This year's fund-raising event would be remembered for years to come.

Now if she could just get Harlan to answer the phone.

Chapter Sixteen

"It's time to go."

James strove for a firm yet gentle tone with the traumatized Jenny.

"You don't get it. They'll catch us and kill us."

How must it feel to be sixteen years old and think you're forever doomed to a life of sexual slavery? To not be able to see help when it was in front of your very eyes?

He took her hand. "We're going. Whatever it takes, I'm going to make sure you leave here and never come back. I don't want to force you, but if that's what I need to do, so be it."

"No." She shrank further from him. "You can't make me and if—"

Enough. He'd wasted a good five minutes trying to gain her cooperation and it wasn't working. James quickly uncuffed her leg irons, then put one arm under her knees and the other across her back, lifting her effortlessly. Jenny gasped and he placed a finger against her lips. "Not another word," he said sternly.

She blinked at him and slowly nodded. It hurt to use that tone with her, but her life was more important than hurt feelings. He crossed the room with the light burden in his arms, relieved tonight was almost over.

James started up the steps, but paused on the third rung. Sharp, staccato footsteps sounded above, from behind the door. Not the soft padding Charlotte made with her flats. The steps grew louder.

Jenny whimpered and turned her face into his chest, afraid of who it might be.

He wasn't so thrilled himself. His only options were to turn back and hide Jenny while he attacked their confronter—or push ahead at full speed and perhaps catch the guard off balance. Too late to retreat, he decided. Press on.

James plowed forward, but Jenny had a different reaction to the danger. She reached her hands out to either side, clinging to the walls in an attempt to slow him down. She twisted and squirmed in his arms, surprisingly feisty. The desperate always managed to draw strength when panicked.

A figure appeared at the top of the stairs— tall, dark and deadly.

"What's this?" Maddie asked with a hiss.

It looked like Maddie, same red outfit and elegant veneer, but her eyes were bereft of even a speck of human warmth. They crackled with aggrieved outrage. She didn't wait for an answer. "You're not going anywhere with my property."

She raised a pistol at them. "Turn around and go downstairs."

If Jenny wasn't in his arms, he'd take his chances—rush Maddie and knock her to the ground. But she was, and he'd do anything to keep her safe.

"Be reasonable, Mrs. Stowers. Your home's crawling with law enforcement and they'll be here at any moment."

Where the hell was Harlan? There'd been plenty of time for Charlotte to have alerted him. His skin flushed hot, then cold. Had something happened to Charlotte?

"Bullshit," she said flatly.

The profanity startled him. He'd thought her much too cultured and uptight to be coarse. "Nobody's coming to save either of you. Now move it."

He wouldn't turn his back on Maddie. Too dangerous. Instead, he slowly descended one step. The longer he delayed entrapment in the basement, the better.

Maddie slammed the door shut and waved her gun. "If I shoot, my aim's at the girl."

Jenny's nails dug through his shirt as she clung to him, her body tense and shaking.

"I'm going," he reassured Maddie. "This is between us. Leave Jenny out of it."

Another step down and still no hint of the cavalry coming to save them. He had to face this alone.

The scent of violets grew strong as Maddie closed in. The clamor of bells spun in his mind, a dizzying vortex of sound.

It was happening all over again. His skin burned as though he was back in Bagram, and his body felt lightweight and unbalanced. He stumbled on the last step and fell backward.

Get it together. Don't hurt Jenny.

He held tight onto her thin frame, absorbing the impact of the cement floor as they tumbled. "Stay behind me," he whispered to Jenny, grabbing her hand and pulling her behind him as he rose to his feet.

Maddie was closing in. He watched as she scanned the room and caught sight of the guards and her husband bound and gagged on the floor.

"Richard?" Her lips curled and her patrician nose flared. "You incompetent fool. What the fuck are you doing down here? You should have sent me to handle this situation."

She waved her gun at the guards, shaking

her head in disgust. "I'll deal with the two of you later."

It was clear who was in control of the trafficking ring. And it wasn't Richard Stowers.

Maddie turned her back on the hapless men and focused her attention on the matter at hand. "It won't do you any good to hide behind the cop, Jenny. Did you really think you were going to get away? Come out and face me. Time I taught you a real lesson in obedience."

James slightly raised his arms to the side, shielding Jenny.

"Give it up, Maddie. Cooperate with me now and it will go better for you."

Her lips curled into a sneer. "That might have worked on these idiots—" she half-turned and waved her gun at Richard and the guards "—but your empty threats don't scare me one iota."

Jenny slipped beneath his right arm and shuffled forward.

"I'll be good," she said around the sobs that wracked her slender body. She dropped to her knees. "Please don't kill us."

"You'll be the first to die. It's you they've been searching for all along. You've been way too much trouble."

She means to gun us both down.

Death permeated the room, settling its dreaded weight on his shoulders. The last seconds of his life played out before him. Had Charlotte made it to safety with the other two girls? He hoped that would be some consolation to her when she discovered their bodies.

"Kill me. Let her go," he said in a last-ditch effort to bargain for Jenny's life. "She's your—" he stumbled over the next word "—*property*. Wouldn't want to miss recouping on your investment, would you?"

He stepped in front of Jenny again as Maddie wavered, clearly weighing the options. Would her greed win over her caution in leaving a witness to his murder? Once Jenny was sold and her ownership transferred to another person, Maddie would no longer have any control over what Jenny might say in the future.

Footsteps pounded down the basement steps and he turned.

Charlotte's voice floated down. "James? Backup's on the way. Where have you—"

She stopped short at the sight of Maddie's gun.

James squeezed his eyes shut momentarily and groaned. Why had she come back downstairs alone? That wasn't the plan.

Maddie frowned. "Hands up. Come on down and join the crowd, Detective Charlotte Helms. Yes, that's right. I know who you are."

Charlotte's eyes widened as she approached,

hands held high. "How long have you known my real identity?"

Charlotte was playing his same game. Keep Maddie engaged, keep her talking, until help arrived.

If they were coming at all.

"Since day one," Maddie said crisply. "That bitch, Karen Hicks, tipped you off about our operation. I intend to make her pay for that, too."

"I don't know anyone by that name," Charlotte said. James admired her loyalty. She'd go to her death and not reveal an informant's name.

"Liar! I thought when Larry fired you, you'd go away. Should have known better."

"Larry?" Charlotte's brows drew together and then smoothed.

"That's right. Your very own Captain Burkhart. He's kept us protected for years."

Damn. Burkhart was in for one serious asskicking—that is, if he ever got out of this freaking basement.

"Son of a bitch," Charlotte breathed.

Heavy footfalls rained down from the room above. Had Harlan arrived with backup—or was it more of the Stowerses' guards?

Maddie's fingers tightened on the trigger and her eyes narrowed.

A chill chased the length of his spine and a roaring pounded in his brain. Holy hell, she was going to kill Charlotte. He recognized the murderous intent in her eyes, the subtle micro-movement of her hands before shooting. He'd witnessed it too many times in combat. With every ounce of willpower he possessed, James tamped down the spiraling sensations that threat-ened to tunnel him back in time and place. Right here, right now, he had to save Charlotte.

He launched his body in front of Charlotte.

Please don't let me be too late.

JAMES'S BODY FLASHED in front of her, blocking Charlotte's view of Maddie's madness.

The crack of gunfire exploded.

Blood. A thin stream of crimson arched up-ward and then fell like droplets of red rain. James pitched forward, landing face-first on the con-crete.

Charlotte swallowed the acrid, burnt scent of gunpowder. She registered the chaos of noise and movement coming from behind her back, and the screams of Jenny curled on the floor, hands over her ears.

Not James. Dear God, no.

She had to touch him, had to know he still breathed. Charlotte dropped to the floor and touched the back of his head, fingers curling over his short, sandy hair.

The whistle of a speeding bullet passed inches

above her head. Unfazed by the danger, she moved her hand lower, down to the familiar, sensitive nape of his neck. Miss Glory had told her to open her heart, but right now her heart felt as if it were breaking. Her fingers probed and explored, finding the beat of his pulse.

He lived.

Hope renewed her mind and heart. They still had a chance to get out of this alive…and together. She homed in on the pandemonium surrounding them, crystallizing her focus.

"Drop it, Stowers."

It was Harlan. And he wasn't alone. A cavalcade of footsteps treaded the wooden floor, and from the corners of her eyes she noted dozens of black shoes and the hems of suit pants.

Maddie retreated a step. "You have no right to be here," she screeched. "This is *my* house. *My* property. *My* land."

Charlotte didn't have to look up and see Maddie's face to know that the woman was losing it. Her shrill voice trembled with panic and fury. Charlotte imagined that Maddie felt trapped as officers pressed in and surrounded her. A criminal mastermind like her might be unhinged at her lack of control in the situation. And that made her very, very dangerous.

Any moment, and Maddie could fire off a

round of bullets, killing many of them before she was shot or taken down.

She had to stop her. Maddie's attention was on Harlan. Now was her chance. Charlotte lunged forward, latching onto Maddie's right ankle. Charlotte yanked at the woman's leg with all her strength.

Maddie shrieked and tried to kick her hand away, but Charlotte held on like a bulldog and pulled on Maddie's leg with both hands.

The elegantly thin Maddie crumpled to the floor, landing on her skinny ass.

Officers stormed from all sides, seizing Maddie's weapon and cuffing her.

"Do you know who I am?" Maddie screamed. "You can't do this. I'll sue you. I'll—"

Charlotte ignored her desperate ramblings and all the mayhem from above. She crawled to Jenny. The girl's stunned, wide-eyed stare was fixed on James's bleeding wound.

"It's my fault," she whispered. "All my fault. He kept trying to get me to go with him, and I wouldn't. And now he's d—"

"Shh. He's not dead," Charlotte assured her, patting Jenny's hand. "But he needs an ambulance, quick."

She left Jenny and hurried over to James.

He moaned and the sound was heavenly to her ears, much as she hated that he was in pain.

She flipped him over onto his back and assessed the damage. All the bleeding stemmed from his right shoulder. It probably hurt like hell, but his heart and vital organs should be fine.

"Here, take this," Harlan said, handing her his jacket. "Medics will be here in a moment. I had them on standby. They said to staunch the bleeding as much as possible until they arrive."

She took the jacket and pressed it against the wound.

James groaned again and his eyelids lifted. Blue eyes shimmered with an equal measure of humor and pain. "Are you trying to kill me?"

"Trying to save you." She cried and laughed through tears. "Don't you ever jump in front of a bullet again. You got that?"

He grimaced and raised up on one elbow. "I don't plan on it."

"Hey, buddy," Harlan said, bending down on his knees. "That was a damn fool thing to do. Don't try to get up. Medics will take you out on a stretcher."

James clenched his jaw and raised to a half-seated position. "I'm fine."

"Like hell you are." Charlotte barely suppressed a snort. James was pale and had lost blood. "Just stay put and—"

"Are Amy and Lisa okay?" he interrupted.

"They're upstairs with Sammy." Charlotte turned and motioned Jenny over. "So is Jenny, or she will be, once she sees you're going to be alright."

James mustered a smile for the young girl. "Told you I wouldn't leave you behind."

Jenny threw himself at him, throwing her arms around his neck. "I'm sorry. It's my fault you got hurt."

Charlotte winced. That hug had to hurt.

James patted her with his uninjured arm. "You're not to blame. Not at all. I'm fine."

Charlotte placed a hand on Jenny's shoulder and drew her away. "He's hurt. Give him a little breathing room," she said lightly.

EMTs clamored down the steps as fast as they could with their bulky stretcher, and Charlotte exhaled a sigh of relief. She hated seeing James in pain. He needed to be stitched up, medicated, and then put to bed.

Maddie's voice rose again over the crowd. "You can't do this to me. Wait until my attorneys hear this…"

Charlotte watched as officers grabbed Maddie by both arms and forced her to move forward.

"Richard, do something," Maddie ordered.

The two guards and Richard Stowers were on

their feet and their gags removed. They were also being read their rights.

"Shut the hell up, Maddie. It's over," Richard snapped.

Jenny hugged her knees to her chin, making herself small, watching Maddie's imminent approach. They'd have to pass close by on their way out. Charlotte moved to shield Jenny from the sight, but Maddie spotted her.

"You little bitch," she screamed, venting her ire at her former captive. "Everything was fine until you came along."

A change swept over Jenny's face. Her eyes flickered from fear to fury and she jumped to her feet, hands clenched into fists. "I hate you," she screamed, her voice even louder than Maddie's. "Hate you, hate you, HATE you."

Maddie blinked. The woman had probably never had a comeuppance before from one of her young, vulnerable victims.

Charlotte wanted to applaud. She'd much rather see her angry than scared. Jenny had spirit. With lots of counseling and her mother's love, she would have the strength to move on with her life.

And hopefully it would be a damn good life.

"Get the Stowerses out of here," Harlan ordered.

His officers hustled Maddie up the steps, her

husband and their two guards close in tow. Maddie didn't say another word.

Charlotte put an arm around Jenny. "You'll never have to see that woman again," she promised. "We'll do all we can to see she stays in prison until she's a very old lady."

Jenny swiped at her eyes and nodded. "I want my mom now."

"Of course." Eagerness burst inside Charlotte like a dam. This was the moment she'd been waiting for ever since she came to Lavender Mountain.

Harlan handed her his cell phone. "Call your friend. She's waited a long time to hear this news."

Charlotte punched in the numbers with shaking hands. "Tanya? Hey, I called because...no, Jenny's not hurt. Just the opposite. Deep breath, hon. I have good news." Charlotte inhaled deeply herself, relieved the ordeal was almost over. She caught James's glance, and he smiled and gave a thumbs-up as an EMT bandaged his wound. For a moment, her lungs choked and she couldn't speak. "Tanya, there's someone here who wants to talk to you."

Wordlessly she handed the phone to Jenny.

"Mom? It's me." Tears, mixed with black mascara, streamed down her heavily made-up cheeks. "Can you come bring me home?"

There wasn't a freaking dry eye in the basement that was still swarming with law enforcement officers—supposedly hardened men and women used to horrendous crimes. Harlan's chest rose and fell and he cleared his throat.

James was suddenly beside her. Stubborn man. He shouldn't be standing at all. But she nestled into his solid warmth. Leaving her job and coming to Lavender Mountain was the best decision she'd ever made.

She'd found Jenny, and so much more.

Chapter Seventeen

James shifted in his seat. The stitches on his right shoulder pinched uncomfortably under his shirt. Not that he'd admit that fact to anyone. Charlotte and Lilah had fussed over him for the last two days and he'd had enough.

"You okay?" Harlan asked, leaning back in his chair.

He groaned. "Don't you start with that, too. I came back to work to escape."

"Nothing but desk duty for you, at least for another couple of weeks." Harlan shoved over a mound of paperwork and gave him an evil grin. "This should be loads of fun for you."

"Yeah, right. Looks like you've let filing go for at least six months. What the hell does Zelda do around here?"

"Everything but filing. She hates it."

James rifled through the papers. Escaping the incessant nursing at home wasn't the only reason he'd returned to the office. But he dallied, reluctant to state his real reason. He changed the subject. "How are Amy and Lisa? Heard any word?"

"Lisa was returned to her home. Unfortunately, Amy tried to commit suicide again. But the good news is that she's been placed in an intensive psychiatric care facility. Hopefully they can put this behind them. How are Jenny and her mom doing?"

"Healing. Glad the nightmare's over, but struggling. It will take time. Charlotte plans on paying them a visit in a couple weeks."

Harlan scowled. "Never would have imagined a human trafficking ring had connections with Lavender Mountain. I'm trying my best to keep Elmore County crime-free, but by the time I clean up one mess, something new and unexpected pops up."

"No need to beat yourself up. The ring hadn't been here long."

Investigation had already revealed that the trafficking ring had been in Lavender Mountain for less than six months. The Stowerses were based in Atlanta, but they'd felt heat from the cops closing in, so they'd decided to cool things off a bit by temporarily switching their base to Falling Rock.

"After all, they'd been running this operation close to a decade in Atlanta," James continued. "There's always something new popping up, too.

It's the nature of the job." And his brother-in-law was doing a damn good job. Credibility in the sheriff's office was finally returning after the disastrous tenure of the old sheriff. "What's the latest on the Stowerses' case?"

"Nothing new there. They're still awaiting trial in Atlanta. The real news is that Captain Larry Burkhart was arrested. Created quite the shake-up in their police department."

"Nothing worse than a dirty cop. After the way he treated Charlotte, I couldn't be happier to hear he's gone."

"I regret that I listened to his nonsense about Charlotte's mental stability."

"You should tell her, not me."

Harlan nodded and cleared his throat. "I intend to."

It was clear that Harlan wasn't looking forward to eating crow, but when he was wrong, he was man enough to own up to it.

"Speaking of Charlotte…" Harlan began. "What are her plans for the future? I'm assuming she'll be offered her old position, given that Burkhart was behind the firing."

"They called this morning. She told them she wasn't interested."

And hadn't he breathed a sigh of relief at that announcement? But Charlotte hadn't said she'd stay with him, either. It was an issue they hadn't discussed yet. But now that he'd recovered from his injury, there was nothing to tie Charlotte to this mountain—or to him.

Their living arrangements were in limbo and it made him uneasy.

Harlan tapped a pencil on his desk, a sure sign he was about to speak on a topic that made him uncomfortable. "You know our office policy. Since you obviously have some kind of—intimate relationship—the two of you can't work together anymore as partners."

"I'm aware. That's another reason I came back to work today." James opened the folder in his lap and took out its only contents—a single typed sheet of paper. "This is my official two-week notice, although if you need me to stay a little longer, I will. But I'm resigning."

He reached across Harlan's desk to hand him the notice, but Harlan didn't take it. James shrugged and let it fall onto the rest of his boss's paperwork.

"There's no need for this. You can both stay on, but work different shifts with different partners."

"The job isn't for me. I appreciate the opportunity, but I'd—"

"You've done damn good work," Harlan interrupted. "What don't you like about it?"

He knew his brother-in-law wasn't going to

take the news well and he hated disappointing him. Harlan had given him a job when he'd returned from military duty, and he was floundering on what he wanted to do next.

"I'm pursuing an old dream. I want to go in business for myself as a carpenter."

"I always knew you were good with your hands...but are you sure about this?"

"Positive." He'd stayed up most of last night, resolving everything in his mind. Nothing like getting shot at point-blank range to make a man rethink his direction in life.

"I may be leaving, but you should keep Charlotte on. She's a fantastic cop."

"Agreed. Although I could find a place for both of you. If you change your mind, the door's always open."

James stood and they shook hands. "Guess I'll be getting a start on all this." He nodded at the stack of papers Harlan had unloaded on him.

"Count on me working you like hell for the next two weeks, buddy."

James grinned. "No problem. I'll see what I can do to get this stuff filed and organized—since you and Zelda obviously won't ever get around to it."

He turned to leave and had almost slipped out the door when Harlan spoke again.

"It's none of my business, but I hope you intend doing your part to get Charlotte to stay on here at Lavender Mountain. Seeing as how you've left me shorthanded. Least you could do."

James narrowed his eyes and gave a slow smile. "I believe you may be as nosy as Lilah."

And with that nonanswer, he made his exit.

"YOU SHOULDN'T BE DRIVING," Charlotte scolded. "You worked late and then insisted on helping me clean up after dinner. Don't you need some rest?"

"Stop fretting over me. I'm fine." James backed the car out of the driveway and eased onto the dark road.

"Where are we going?"

"Nowhere in particular," he lied. "I was cooped up in the house for two days and then spent all day at the office. Thought it'd be nice to get out for a spell."

They settled into a comfortable silence as they traveled up the steep mountain road. A deep peace filled him since he'd turned in his notice. His career path was clear. At least that part of his life was in order.

Charlotte played with a lock of her hair. "I've been thinking—"

"Always dangerous," he teased.

She gave him a hard stare. "I'm going back to Atlanta this weekend."

His chest squeezed tight. "Why?"

"My apartment is a wreck. Remember? I need to clean it up and take care of my bills. You know, all the daily routine stuff that's gone undone."

His chest relaxed a fraction. "A temporary visit, then?"

"For now. The police commissioner asked if I'd meet with him."

His hands tightened on the steering wheel as he rounded a bend. "They really want you back."

"Maybe. Or maybe he wants reassurance that I won't go to the press about the way Burkhart ordered me to quit the case and then fired me when I refused."

The Atlanta news media was having a field day with the news that a high-ranking member of the police department had helped cover up a human trafficking ring.

"When are you leaving? Friday?"

"Bright and early."

Seemed like he was already losing her. Could she really be happy working and living in such a remote area? He didn't want Charlotte to settle. He wanted her to live out all her dreams. And if that meant living in Atlanta, he wouldn't stop her.

The confidence he'd felt earlier vanished. She hadn't told him yet that she loved him. He'd been so sure he'd seen it in her eyes down in the Stowerses' basement after he'd been shot. Had read a desperate concern in her eyes as she'd hovered over him once he'd been shot.

But he might be wrong.

Another silence descended—though this time not as peaceful. James continued up the mountain, then turned onto the familiar dirt driveway. Headlight beams illuminated the charred remnants of his old family cabin.

Charlotte glanced his way, brows raised. "You really want to see this place again? The last time we were here was so sad."

"Not all my memories here are bad ones."

"Right," Charlotte touched his arm. "You grew up in that cabin. I'm sure you had lots of great times."

He pulled around to the back of the yard. Yep, the old metal glider swing remained. He stopped the car and stuffed the keys in his pocket. "But my favorite memory of all is that this is where I first met you."

A delighted grin broke across her face. "Aww…that's so sweet."

"Come on." He got out and headed for the trunk.

"For a minute," she agreed, climbing out. "It's cold out here."

James opened the trunk and pulled out a thick quilt. "I've got you covered."

"Looks like you had this planned from the get-go."

"True," he confessed. He put an arm around her and led her to the glider.

"Did your mom make this quilt?"

"Grandmother. Mom wasn't into all the domestic stuff."

Charlotte sat down and he tucked the quilt around her legs before sitting beside her.

She giggled. "How could I forget the first time we met? That look on your face when you ordered me to stop running—so ferocious."

"Of course it was. You pointed a gun at me."

"Because I thought you were one of them and had come to finish me off."

A grin split his face. "Freezing cold and you had on nothing but an oversize camouflage shirt and black panties. All long, sexy legs, wild red hair and an attitude."

She jostled his side with her elbow. "Is that why you followed me everywhere and wouldn't leave me alone? You lusted after my body?"

"You were a mystery. One I had to solve."

"It's what makes you a good officer."

"About that... I turned in my two-week notice today."

Surprised widened her teal-green eyes. "Why?"

"It's not for me. I've been longing to go back to my old job. To work with my hands again."

"Doing what?"

"Carpentry."

He studied her face closely. Carpentry wasn'
exactly a sexy kind of job, and it might take some
time before he became established in the community. For some women, that could be a rea
turnoff.

"A carpenter," she murmured thoughtfully
"You're full of surprises. I should have guessec
with the whittling piece at your house. If that':
what makes you happy, then you should absolutely go for it."

His gaze drifted to what remained of the burn
pine structure. "My first job will be to tear dowr
what's left of Dad's cabin and rebuild it into a
new home."

"I love that idea, James." She paused a few
heartbeats. "And I love you."

The tension in his shoulders relaxed. Charlotte
loved him. They could figure the rest out later—
together. He stroked her hair and ran his finger:
over the delicate features of her face.

"Forever?" he asked quietly, hardly daring to
breathe.

Her teal eyes sparkled and shimmered. "Yes
And I promise I'll never run away from you again.'

Epilogue

Charlotte's breath caught at the stunning vista. A woman couldn't ask for a more perfect wedding day. Dogwoods blossomed on top of Lavender Mountain and the lush greenness of the forest contrasted with the turquoise sky. To think by summer's end she'd be living here, waking up each morning next to James and admiring this gorgeous view from their new home.

Her gaze sought his through the throng of well-wishers. He was deep in conversation with Sammy and Harlan. The threesome looked so arresting in their tuxes that her breath caught. Of course, James was the most handsome by far. How lucky was she?

As if attuned to her every nuance, James lifted his eyes and scanned the crowd until they settled on her. A slow, sexy grin lit his face.

Lilah was suddenly by her side. "Pretty impressive, huh?" she asked.

"He is," Charlotte murmured, gaze still locked on her groom.

Lilah laughed and slapped her arm. "I'm talking about the cabin, silly. Not my brother."

Charlotte wrenched her gaze from James and stared at his handiwork. The burnt remains of his dad's old place had been torn down, and a new home for the two of them was coming along at a quick pace. James had hired a crew and worked sunup until sundown, returning home every night sweaty and dirty, with a huge smile lighting his face. And he slept soundly at night, the insomnia a thing of the past.

"It doesn't have the grandeur of a Falling Rock mansion, but it'll do, right?"

Again she had to snap her thoughts back to the conversation at hand. "It's perfect."

Lilah hugged her. "I'm so glad you're marrying my brother. I haven't seen him this happy since before his first overseas tour of duty. You're good for him."

"And he's good for me. I was lonely and totally burned out working undercover." She hadn't even known how miserable she was until she met James and came to Lavender Mountain.

"I only wish Dad and Darla were here to see your wedding. And the new house."

"Me, too." She and James had talked about it just last night. His father would have been proud of James's accomplishments. "This work has been good for James. It's as if he's laying to rest the ghosts from his past with every board he cuts."

"What's this about ghosts of the past?" James was beside her, and Lilah waved goodbye, strolling over to Harlan and Sammy.

"Nothing. From here on out, it's nothing but new beginnings," she promised.

"No second thoughts about marrying a carpenter?" His voice was light and teasing, but his eyes hinted at worry.

"Not when you've built us this gorgeous house complete with custom cabinets and bookshelves." She winked. "Who am I to complain? You should be the worried one. I work crazy hours with Sammy and I've made plenty of enemies over the years."

"You're safe with me. Forever." James lifted her left hand, and her engagement ring sparkled in the late afternoon sun.

"I know," she whispered.

He lifted a strand of her red hair and smiled. "Glad it's back to its fiery color. It suits you." Then he kissed her. It started out as a quick press of the lips, but he deepened the kiss and she was lost in the moment.

Cheers and whistles from the wedding guests brought her back to reality. Before she could pull away, James whisked her into his arms and spun her around.

In a dizzying whirl, she saw them all there— her mom and dad and brothers, Harlan and all her coworkers, even Tanya and Jenny had come for the celebration. Finally, she was at home. At peace. In a place where she could plant roots and spend the rest of her life. Lavender Mountain was the haven she hadn't even known she was seeking.

Miss Glory had told her to open her heart, and at last she finally had.

* * * * *

Get 2 Free Books,
Plus 2 Free Gifts—
just for trying the *Reader Service!*